# Sutra
## & Other Stories

## Simin Daneshvar

Translated from the Persian by
Hasan Javadi and Amin Neshati

Mage Publishers
Washington, D.C.
1994

Front and back jacket painting is *A Seated Princess*, attributed to Mohammad-Sharif Musawwir, Iran, circa 1600. Courtesy of the Arthur M. Sackler Gallery, Smithsonian Institution, Washington, D.C. S1986.304

**Library of Congress Cataloging-in-Publication Data**

Danishvar, Simin, 1921–
Sutra and other stories / Simin Daneshvar; translated by
Hassan Javadi and Amin Neshati. — 1st ed.
p. cm.   ISBN 0-934211-42-6
1. Danishvar, Simin, 1921–  —Translations into English.
I. Javadi, Hasan. II. Neshati, Amin. III. Title.
PK6561.D263S88 1994   891' .5533—dc20

First Edition
Printed and Manufactured in USA

Mage books are available through independent bookstores or directly from the publisher toll-free (800) 962-0922 or (202) 342-1642.

# Contents

# Potshards

Farajollah turned to the headman and said that he'd heard seven governments had pooled their money and bought up all the treasure maps and scanned them. They'd hired a bunch of people who'd be coming any day now to dig up the treasures from the land. Then he called my brother, Mohsen, and said, "A cup of sweet tea, boy. Charge it to the headman!" I took off to spread the news among the village boys. They in turn told their fathers, and soon the coffee-house was crowded. The men sat on the cots and the boys sat on the ground at their fathers' feet and everybody's eyes were glued to Farajollah's lips.

Farajollah said, "Yes, I've heard they'll come here and go to the mounds and dig and dig until they strike a marble coffin. In the marble coffin there'll be a dragon sleeping on treasure . . . "

Uncle Hosayn Ali Sarbaneh cut Farajollah off, and now everybody's eyes were glued to Uncle Hosayn Ali's lips as he said, "Heaven help you, man, what treasure? Haven't our own kids dug enough? Take it from me, these folks are looking for something, like the Jews. And they're not going to hire us. They'll bring their own people."

Farajollah stood up and raised his voice. "So I left my peddling business for nothing, eh? I heard it with my own two ears from the gendarme at the caravanserai. They'll come and they'll dig up the mounds and they'll hire us."

Uncle Hosayn Ali took his chibouk out of his jacket pocket and said, "And when the Jews came, it was the butchery business you left."

Farajollah said, "Wasn't I the first person who said they were bringing in expert Jews from Israel to build Israelabad here? Whatever I've said so far has happened."

Uncle Hosayn Ali pulled out his tobacco pouch and buried his chibouk in it. "They're all looking for oil, anyway. Those deep wells the Jews dug were for oil. It's not as if we don't have water from aqueducts."

Everybody was quiet, listening eagerly to Farajollah and Uncle Hosayn Ali's talk. My brother was hobbling around, serving tea. Farajollah remained standing. He picked up where he had left off: "Never mind about the Jews, now.

These ones who are coming are like us. Why not give it to you straight? The gendarme at the caravanserai has sent you all a message. He says the wages have already been fixed—ten-and-a-half *tuman*s a day for the men, six *tuman*s a day for the boys, four *tuman*s for the little ones. They pay according to your birth certificate. The higher the age, the higher the pay."

The headman complained—why hadn't he come out with it sooner? Everyone was abuzz with talk. The boys were happy, the fathers happier. Everybody ordered tea. My brother was passing me the tea glasses and I put them in front of the fathers, even in front of the sons. The women and girls never came to the coffeehouse, but their handwoven rugs were spread on the cots. The Jews had so far bought two rugs woven by Naneh Tajmah.

The headman turned to me and said, "Khorrang, you will take your brother's birth certificate."

Farajollah said, "They'll make me foreman. I'm more in the know about these things than anybody else. It's not for nothing I've drunk the waters everywhere—the Fakhrabad waters, the Shah waters, the Embassy waters." Then he turned to my brother Mohsen and repeated, "A tea with sugar cubes, boy!" and, laughing, "Charge it to the headman!"

I knew my brother's leg was hurting again. His limp was more pronounced than it had been earlier in the evening.

He placed one hand on his knee, took a half turn, and went over to the samovar.

The headman turned to the boys and said, "From now on I forbid anybody to go to the mounds. And don't let on to the Sakezabad kids. After all, these people aren't going to hire more than thirty or forty laborers."

Every afternoon after school and on weekends, my schoolmates and I would go to the mounds and drill and dig and delve and find a mass of potshards. We'd pull from the earth as many human and animal arm and leg bones and skulls as you can imagine and just leave them there. Weekends, the kids from Sakezabad would also show up. They'd come looking for leg bones. Any leg bones they found, they'd stuff into their pockets and take to their own village and play at bones. As my brother said, they were "bonesters." They were experts at pilfering walnuts and grapes and onions and potatoes. And now, would you believe it! God had sent an earthquake to all the villages in Zahra, but had spared Sakezabad—marvel at His work! Maybe it was recompense for the three mosques they had built there, or recompense for the shrine of Ali Akbar, or maybe—as they themselves said—it was because they never missed their prayers.

The year the earthquake struck, I was all of three years old. Naneh Tajmah had told me time and time again about how the ground had moved and cracked and how the ceiling beam had fallen diagonally and I had been saved by the skin of my teeth; and how my brother, who had positioned himself to protect me, had gotten his leg stuck under the rubble. She'd told me so many times I thought I remembered it myself.

Naneh Tajmah would say, "That night neither you nor your brother had any sleep till morning. Your brother was in pain, and you were crying for your mother." She said that she had told us all the stories she knew, sung us all the lullabies she knew, but it had been no use. Now whenever Naneh Tajmah sings a lullaby she cries, in memory of our folks, in memory of her own folks, in memory of all the village folk who had perished under the rubble.

After the earthquake, at the crack of dawn, Uncle Hosayn Ali came for us. He saw—praise God—not a thing was wrong with me. He set my brother's leg and asked Naneh Tajmah to tell us a story. Naneh Tajmah told the one about the pigeons: "Two pigeons were sitting in a tree. One of them flew away." And even Uncle Hosayn Ali burst into tears.

We'd go and dig and dig on the mounds. Sometimes God would lend a hand and we'd find a complete earthen bowl or a plate or a tallow lamp with painted talismans. We'd either give them to the headman, who'd give us two *rial*s, or to our school teacher, who'd give us two *tuman*s if he had it, or we'd wait for Ali Asghar, the middleman for the Americans, to come from the city.

We'd dug and delved so much that I'd gradually come to recognize what kind of vessel suited the traveling types, especially Ali Asghar, or the Jews of Israelabad. If I got my hands on a vessel of that kind, I'd quietly hide it under my worsted jacket. And when Kablai Asadollah, the coffeehouse man, was out of sight, I'd hand it to my brother. He'd hide it somewhere safe and wait for fate to send a traveler his way.

Every night, I'd go to the coffeehouse. Kablai Asadollah had told my brother, who was his busboy, that he could give me tea and bread and cheese, but if I got a hankering for eggs or *abgusht*, I'd have to pay. My brother would sneak me everything, though. Stealing grapes and walnuts was no problem, either. Of course, every night when my brother had to settle accounts, there'd be a bowl of stew or a couple of eggs missing. Sometimes things would grow into a quarrel, but in the end Kablai Asadollah would forgive him. Every night, I'd sleep right there in my brother's arms. My brother's hair smelled of tobacco, and I'd lay my head on his breastbone. And you should have heard us talk! How we talked!

We'd count our money. We decided to buy two young goats and tie them at the coffeehouse gate. "The goats will grow big," I'd tell myself. "We'll sell them and then I'll take my brother to the city and have his leg operated on. Then he'll marry Uncle Hosayn Ali's daughter and the girl will get pregnant and have a child. There'll be none of that earthquake business. I'll hold my brother's baby in my arms and kiss it and fondle it and prattle to it . . .

"We'll buy two lottery tickets from Ali Asghar, middleman for the Americans, and our luck, which according to Naneh Tajmah lies smoldering in the ashes, will wake up with a yawn and we'll be winners. With the money we'll go to Qazvin—no, why Qazvin? Now that we've won we'll go to Tehran. I'll study to be a doctor, just like Dr. Dana'ifard Ebrahimabadi, who's built an orchard and sunk a deep well and carries around a black bag and wears glasses."

Dr. Dana'ifard Ebrahimabadi couldn't operate on my brother's leg, but I'd be able to. I'd do it right away, and as soon as he recovered we'd get him married and throw a housewarming for him.

I mentioned that my brother's leg had been trapped under the rubble as he'd tried to save me when the earthquake struck. That's how a seven-year-old goes lame—that is, the boy's leg breaks and Uncle Hosayn Ali sets it badly. Well, Uncle Hosayn Ali had been very busy that day. He'd set the arms and legs of children and grown-ups. So many children and grown-ups had been buried under rubble. My mama and papa and aunt and uncles were also buried under rubble. They got to them too late; all of them had died. So there was the burial of so many dead on the one hand, and the setting of children's and grown-ups' arms and legs on the other. They'd hired a mullah from the city to say the prayer for the dead.

My brother and I had grown up passed around among the village folk and Kablai Asadollah and Uncle Hosayn Ali and Naneh Tajmah. Until recently, Naneh Tajmah would still tell us the story: "There were two pigeons sitting in a tree. One of them flew away." We were scrawny kittens, feeding at this one's and that one's table until we became conscious beings. We even went to school. And we learned the prayer to ward off disaster. Whenever the Raz or Miyeh wind picked up, we'd get scared and say the prayer against disaster. My brother studied six grades and then became a busboy to the coffeehouse man; in our village, Ebrahima-bad, we had only six grades, and my brother, with his crippled leg, couldn't walk in the mornings to Bu'in Zahra and come back in the afternoons. But I could, and I had registered. Next year I'd enter the seventh grade.

The headman explained to everyone what they were to do and not to do. When all the plans had been made, every-body left. My brother and Kablai Asadollah settled their accounts, and there was no quarreling this time. Finally, it was just me and my brother. But my brother was just sitting there by the samovar, exhausted. He wouldn't get up to close up the coffeehouse and lock the door from the inside and shut the windows so the Raz wouldn't blow inside and so we could sleep in each other's arms and I could lay my head on his breastbone and we could talk about the goats and the lottery ticket.

I said, "Not going to bed, brother?"

He said, "My leg hurts. I got up too fast to pour the tea. There's a pain shooting through my whole body now." I sat on the floor and rubbed my brother's kneecap. He pushed my hand away and said, "You go to bed." I asked, "Aren't you going to shut the door and windows?" He said, "That's my business, not yours. You go to bed. Tomorrow I'll give you my birth certificate." I did as he said, but I knew that until my brother came to bed I'd have no sleep.

Now just picture this. They come to you and say, "Khorrang, dig away!" And you dig and dig until you strike a royal jar. When you lift the top of the jar what do you see? Great God! What quantities of gold and jewelry! You betray nothing to them, of course. You simply replace the top of the jar very quietly and cover it with a stone or something to mark the spot. You mark it in various ways so you don't forget what's where. Then you go someplace else and dig and toss out potshards—bones and potshards. And when they come you say, "Gentlemen, I'm really sorry, what you see is what I found." They believe you, of course. They take you somewhere else to dig. Then one day, when they're not on the mound, you pretend to have a stomachache and don't show up to help Uncle Hosayn Ali in the fields. No, God, I have it! You wait for winter to come, then don't go to school. Instead, you swipe Kablai Asadollah's saddlebag, and when no one's looking, you go to the mound . . . no, God, wait a minute! You go at night. You have a lantern, right? You stuff all the gold and jewels in the saddlebag and you bring it and put it under your head and your brother's like a pillow. When the bus arrives in the morning, you both get on and go to the city. Now suppose someone smells a rat: you throw the bag over your shoulder and take off and go and go until you end up in Tehran. You return and take your brother to the hospital so they can reset his leg. You your-self attend high school in the city. There they go as high as the twelfth grade. Even higher.

My brother came to bed and turned his back to me. I moved close and said, "What if I hit the marble coffin, brother? I'll take you to Tehran so they can reset your leg." He said, "Go to sleep. There's no hope for resetting this leg of mine. Didn't Dr. Dana'ifard Ebrahimabadi say so?" I said, "If we get the treasure, we'll buy a car just like the doctor's. We'll hire a chauffeur, too. You marry Uncle Hosayn Ali's daughter, Morvarid, and I'll marry her sister, Golabtun. Just like Dr. Dana'ifard Ebrahimabadi, we'll put our wives in the car so they can look at the village women and laugh just for the heck of it."

"Go to sleep, kid," my brother snapped. "Let me get some rest."

Why lie to you? All of us went to the mounds at first hoping to find the treasure. We'd dig with pickaxes all afternoon until it got dark. Even the Sakezabad kids were afraid of the dark, because Farajollah Ghorbati had said the entire area was haunted by jinn. But the headman would say, "The jinn leave us alone." The headman had entrusted his pickax to me. Once everyone had left, I'd stay behind and dig. Well, if the first layer is broken pottery, you probably have to dig to the bottom before you pull up the jewelry. And these bones? Well, they mean that other men have come here in search of royal jars and fallen victim to the earthquake right here when it struck. I, for one, wasn't afraid of any jinni or wind or corpse. It's just that the wind wouldn't let me light a candle. I bought a lantern from Farajollah, and I'd place it in the shelter of the rise in the mound and I'd dig. But no matter how much I dug, I never hit a coffin in which there'd be a dragon sleeping. There were lots of snakes, of course. There were lizards, too, but not in the coffins. Now, as Farajollah said, seven governments had pooled their money and hired a bunch of people to dig and dig and strike a marble coffin, and they had actually hired us to do the digging for them. And instead of digging they called it "excavation." Well, what does it matter?

17

First, an old, white-haired man with bright black eyes dismounted from the jeep, then a man in a foreign hat, then a blue-eyed bearded guy, then a man in glasses, then a mottle-face, and finally a tallish man who'd lost his hair. It wasn't long before a bus pulled up and a bunch of boys much bigger than my brother stepped out. Then I figured the time for the Imam's appearance was near, because almost half of the group were girls, but they'd turned themselves into boys. They wore trousers and jackets and had rimmed hats and glasses.

All of us village folk had turned out—kids, grown-ups, women, men. We'd been preparing ourselves for several days. Most folks went to the bath or drew water from Dr. Dana'ifard Ebrahimabadi's deep well and soaped and lathered themselves. Farajollah Ghorbati set up with a loincloth and a razor and shaved the men's heads and faces. The womenfolk washed their men's clothes. They shook out the coffeehouse rugs and swept and mopped the Ebrahimabad school. Only Uncle Hosayn Ali was busy with his own farm. He didn't go to the bath and didn't shave his whiskers, even though it was the peak of summer and not yet time for the harvest. Well, he could at least do his weeding.

We'd planted onions and potatoes that the Raz couldn't find underground and scorch. Now, as luck would have it, it had been two days and two nights since the Raz had really picked up. The wind kicked up sand and dust that chased you from behind or hit you smack in the chest and, before you knew it, it had raised a curtain of dust and come crashing down all over the travelers. We all knew it would burn up the saplings the Jews had planted. But, as Uncle Hosayn Ali said, it was their own fault. They should have known better and planted pistachios; what was the use of grafting golden and red apples?

The white-haired man, the headman, and Uncle Hosayn Ali Sarbaneh led the way, with the travelers following behind, and we—men, women, children—following them. Never in our village had so many people set off at once together, not even during the *ta'ziyeh* days when we went to hear the religious opera in Sakezabad. Only my brother was missing from the scene. When I said good-bye to him that morning, he cried.

We walked on until we came to the first mound. They started naming them. The first one they called Sakezabad Hill; maybe they liked the sound of it, because the mound was actually closer to us, the Ebrahimabad folk. After the naming, they made Farajollah Ghorbati foreman and the white-haired man said he'd make us apprentices. When they started to measure the ground and the mound, we covered our faces and laughed in our sleeves. The white-haired man was standing in the middle, the travelers around him, and we behind them—just like the street show in Bu'in Zahra. He turned to the folks and said, "For some two, two-and-a-half meters the mound is unstable. First we're going to do pottery picking." I knew what "unstable" meant. Just a month and a half ago in our spelling test I'd written it with an *o* first, then crossed it out and written *unstabel* above it. That night, my brother had been really nervous I'd flunk and not get a sixth-grade diploma. Early next morning, I'd gone to the school to see our teacher. I waited a long time before he finally arrived. He said, "If you've brought me something, I should tell you I don't have any money today. Ali Asghar is here. Go sell it to him." No, I hadn't come to sell anything. I asked him and he wrote it on the board for me: *unstable*. He said, "That's how the word is spelled. It means when someone is nervous." Well, we'd badly torn up the bowels of the mound; maybe it was nervous.

The white-haired man really put on a spectacle. Then he began marking. The blue-eyed bearded guy wrote our names and said, "Bring your birth certificates tomorrow." We all had brought ours, and I'd brought my brother's. He took a hard look at me and wrote down my name. I said my brother wasn't there, he was watching the coffeehouse. Besides, even if he had been there, they wouldn't have put him down; how could he walk all this way through the Raz? Sometimes the Raz wind would blow on one side and the

Miyeh wind on the other. The travelers' baggage and things arrived and they set up camp in the school.

The cock was crowing next morning when we went to work. I found myself under the blue-eyed bearded guy's command. He told the girls in trousers to draw lines on the flat ground, and Farajollah hammered stakes at the two ends of the lines. To the end of each line, which was five meters long—sometimes longer—we tied string. Each line was about half a meter apart from the next one. Then he told us boys to put whatever potshards we found into a handbarrow and bring them to the flat ground. He called it "pottery picking." We cackled. These were the very same shards we'd left lying around. He said, "Some of these earthenware pieces are worth hundreds of thousands." We kids were splitting our sides with laughter. Then he made one of the girls our leader. The girl was much uglier than Morvarid, Uncle Hosayn Ali's daughter, and much older too. Besides, she was tawny. She'd be no good for my brother. Until noon all she did was hand us shards and we put them on the ground between the lines: handles in one place, lids and covers in another, and vessel parts still some-where else. First came what she called coarse pottery, then more delicate pieces, arranged according to the patterns of the talismans drawn on the shards. Mostly the talismans showed goats and cows and sheep. But just as goats and cows are dumb, so were we dumb. The girl, our leader, would say, "This piece of pottery resembles the pottery from such-and-such a place, and that one resembles the pottery from this-and-that place." And she'd say, "These patterns are goats and cows." Other than their horns and tails, though, they had no resemblance to goats and cows. In drawing class I myself drew much better goats and cows. In one of the lined strips, we arranged human and animal bones. A short, bearded man was put in charge of the bones. The amazing thing is, they themselves didn't find any of it funny.

The girl's work consisted of marking the shards with codes. And boy, was she bad-tempered! If we put a shard in the wrong place she'd smack us on the wrist. In return for this game I got a wage of six *tuman*s that afternoon—of course, only because of my brother's birth certificate, or I would have gotten only four *tuman*s, like Ramazan. It was a good, easy game, except that the sun was hot, the Raz blew hot dust into your face and eyes, and I got five smacks on the wrist.

How we laughed that night in the coffeehouse! How we laughed! The headman had come too, but he wasn't laughing. Farajollah had killed a sheep to send the meat to them. There were about forty of them. We scrounged up some money and bought a few legs and pieces of liver from Farajollah, and, no offense to you, had us an excellent broth. Naneh Tajmah had baked bread—what good, fresh bread!

The second day they kept saying, "We'll sound the depth here, we'll sound the depth there." We thought sounding the depth must be a very difficult thing to do. We were waiting for them to level the ground, but finally, in the middle of nowhere, they drew a line about one meter long and Farajollah fell to work on the mound with pickax and shovel. He dug away, and they taught him how to dig without moving the potshards. Farajollah would get tired and put aside his shovel and wipe the sweat from his brow, which would get muddy because his hands were dusty. Then he'd begin to sing: "It's me and the shovel and Afrasiab's battlefield." This Ghorbati man was literate and could recite poetry from memory. They'd correct him, but he'd still repeat his mistakes. He also wore a wrist watch. He was in Qazvin virtually every day, because lately he'd taken up peddling. He'd also gone to Tehran numerous times. He himself used to say he'd drunk the waters everywhere—Fakhrabad waters, the Shah waters, the Embassy waters. Anyway, he'd drunk all kinds of water, and because he knew all sorts of things, they'd made him foreman over all the workers, boys and men alike. The year before last, in the fight over the water when Ramazan's father had taken a shovel to the back of that youth, Isa the Turk, and we'd all watched as Isa the Turk met his end, Uncle Hosayn Ali had been away; he'd gone to Mashhad on pilgrimage. Farajollah and the headman had been the only ones who'd gone to

fetch the gendarme from the caravanserai at Mohammadabad Khorreh. Then they'd gone to Tehran and testified that
the murderer had been Ramazan's father, and after all this
time Ramazan's father is still in jail. Once a week Ramazan
gets on the bus and goes to Tehran, sometimes for free and
sometimes having to pay. He's learned all the nooks and
crannies. He slips through the legs of the policemen and
other visitors and, by whatever means, gets to his father.
He's my age and in my class.

Every so often, the blue-eyed bearded guy would gather
the boys and girls around himself and teach them things.
They'd write quickly in their big notebooks and would even
look at each other's writing, but the blue-eyed bearded guy
wouldn't scold them. They called him "doctor." I wanted to
take him to the coffeehouse so he could examine my
brother's leg. But he was doing needless busywork, worrying
about everything, thinking and talking of nothing but reaching virgin soil. From what he said, I gathered that these
potshards had once been pots belonging to folks who had
passed on, people who lived in the neighborhood of our village thousands of years ago. The tasks he gave us were easy,
but the words he used were difficult. Now he was talking of
breastwork and strata. Farajollah would learn more quickly
than the rest of us. He'd put aside his shovel, wipe the sweat
off his forehead and say, "Babri Eqbal gave me a breastwork.
He's struck some remains, or a skeleton, or ashes, or a rub-

bish heap." It depended on what he had struck. The two of them named the layers every two fingerbreadths apart. The blue-eyed bearded guy would mark each layer and fix its age and say, "The pottery from this layer resembles what you'll find in Cheshmeh Ali," for example, but it seemed too much for him to say "Ali, upon him be greetings." Apparently, the dowry for girls thousands of years ago was these very same earthen pots—unlike Uncle Hosayn Ali's daughters, whose mama buys them copper and things, and both of whom wear gold bangles.

The blue-eyed bearded guy was marking all the layers. He'd finished with three of them when they hit a longish lozenge. These had been named "cigarette lozenges" a while ago. Praise God! The impressions of the fingers of the men two or three thousand years ago were still on the lozenges. The blue-eyed bearded guy was so happy I thought he'd struck the marble coffin. But what do you know—this was a sign that there had been home-building; they'd uncovered the houses of the dead from a few thousand years ago. In this fourth layer they also found a skull-and-bones flag and the shell of a tortoise. They taught Farajollah how to chisel away gently with a pickax to reveal rooms, walls, steps, and courtyards of the dead from thousands of years ago, so they could see what it was like. Then they cordoned off the rooms with string so the spirits of the dead wouldn't come after them at midnight. They probably also sang "I Sealed up His Tongue" and blew around themselves a few times, but they kept their singing low so we wouldn't hear.

The men would usually come to the coffeehouse at night. Every now and then, the boys would also come. Ramazan was there every night. We talked of nothing but them, and my brother would sit and put his hand on his kneecap and listen. Sometimes he'd put his head on his knee. One time he asked Farajollah, "Are they going to leave when winter comes?" Farajollah said, "I'm hoping to God they'll continue to work in the winter. God, I hope they find something they can sink their teeth into so they'll stay here permanently."

Uncle Hosayn Ali said, "Let anyone say what he wants, when they lose hope of finding oil they'll leave, like the Jews who came and dug all those deep wells and dried up our aqueducts. They spread nylon over their tomato crop to throw us off, now they want to pack up and go."

"At any rate," Farajollah said, "They taught you cleft grafting, didn't they?"

"Yes, they did," said Uncle Hosayn Ali.

Farajollah said, "These are your own people. They want nothing with oil. When they hit virgin soil they'll stop. They were saying so themselves."

My brother asked, "When are they going to hit virgin soil?" He said the words and then left the coffeehouse. I knew he was going to limp toward the little stream that came from the doctor's deep well and sit there and cry his heart out. Then he'd wash his face and come back.

Uncle Hosayn Ali refused to work for the travelers. He only sold them his potatoes and onions. Whatever price he asked, they paid.

Gradually, the Sakezabad kids got themselves involved and the people hired them, because now they had attacked three mounds. They had named all of them, too. One was Graveyard Hill, which was a graveyard for all the people who had lived in the first mound. Another was Zagheh Hill, which was the graveyard of more ancient people. The big black village dog also showed up. Every day he'd come to the base of the mound and bark at the blue-eyed bearded guy, and when he stroked the dog on the head it would wag its tail. Ali Asghar, the middleman for the Americans, would also come and engage in small talk, then go and sit in a corner to watch. Now Ali Asghar was looking for treasure maps and old books. There was no more talk of a whole earthenware pot with talismans. It had been some two or three days since he'd bought the old and tattered *Book of Kings* from the coffeehouse. Kablai Asadollah said, "I'll go to Tehran and buy a new one."

I saved up enough that I was able to buy a frisky little goat in installments from the village shepherd. I tied him at the coffeehouse gate. Every day I'd go and gather up all the cantaloupe and watermelon and cucumber rind that they'd thrown away and bring it to my goat. The folks on the mound also ate cucumbers and cantaloupes and melons.

We'd hear rumors about a lady who was expected to come and see our mounds and barren desert and leave her grief in the desert and go back. One day a short, white-skinned old woman came, wearing a foreign cloth hat and looking like a foreigner herself. The old woman also wore pants and dark glasses and was dressed head to toe in black. Everybody greeted her. I guess the lady was some school superintendent or something. She greeted everybody back and made small talk. That day Sakezabad Hill wasn't very crowded. Most of the girls and boys and workers had gone to Graveyard Hill and were moving the corpses around.

The blue-eyed bearded guy spread a new burlap sack on the floor of the little room where the long cigarette lozenges had been found. He said to her, "Please have a seat." The room was in the shade, but all the other seats were spread under the sun. The Raz wind piled layer over layer of dust.

But the lady didn't go down the steps; she just stood looking at the wasteland while the wind pushed dust into her hair. She looked at the markings, counted the layers, and sighed. She said, "A thousand years of human life contained in a few fingerbreadths of dust, within a strip of dust." We'd all left off from work, looking intently at the lady. The blue-eyed bearded guy was walking beside her and talking to her. They talked a lot, but we couldn't hear. Finally, the lady came close to us and said aloud, "Life here goes on pretty much as in prehistory . . . " These people were all talking about prehistory, and at the end of it all we couldn't figure out what year this prehistory was. Maybe there wasn't any year involved—I don't know. Anyway, the lady and the blue-eyed bearded guy stood over me, and the blue-eyed bearded guy put his hand on my shoulder and said, "This is Khorrang." I jumped up and Madam squatted next to me and asked, "How old are you?" I said, "Seventeen." The blue-eyed bearded guy said, "Your brother's seventeen. Tell Madam the truth." I said nothing. Madam put her hand on my head and looked at me closely. "You were right," she said. "His eyes are the color of the ocean at sundown." I can't tell you how embarrassed I was. No woman had ever put her hand on my head, not even Naneh Tajmah, and no one had ever commented on the color of my eyes.

Maybe the old lady didn't understand that she wasn't supposed to be on familiar terms with me. Then she said, "The skin on his cheeks is like the skin of a ruptured pomegranate," or some such thing. I was about to knock her hand away and run, but I didn't. She seemed so sorrowful. "It seems like they've drawn his eyebrows with gold water." She wasn't about to let up. Now she put her hand on my shoulder and said, "Khorrang, take your jacket off. The wind is hot." What was it to her that I should take off or leave on my tattered worsted jacket? Of course, my worsted jacket had gotten very tight. It was full of holes, and the knots had broken off in places. However many times Naneh Tajmah darned it, it was no use. Some other place would break off. It was feminine too. After the earthquake, the city people had come to Ebrahimabad for relief work. Some pious, devout lady, her face glowing with light, had taken off her worsted jacket and put it on my brother, like an overcoat. Early on, my brother would spread the worsted jacket like a blanket over both of us. Later, Naneh Tajmah took in the cuffs and the hem and the collar, and as my brother grew, she let it out. Soon my brother passed it on to me. I loved it so much I wore it in summer or winter.

Madam sat on the new burlap sack. The fellow who was like a foreigner brought a whole bunch of potshards and glue and a brush and put them in front of Madam, and she began gluing them together. Their work consisted of this: putting the potshards together to make cracked vessels with talismans on them. Then they'd look at them and praise and congratulate each other.

That night, everyone in the coffeehouse knew Madam had come, and they were talking about her. Farajollah said, "I, for one, didn't like her. She sighed so much and said such nonsense. I couldn't tell whose friend she was." Uncle

Hosayn Ali was displeased and upbraided him. "Don't talk like that," he said. "I know Madam. The year of the earthquake she and her husband came to these parts and brought us provisions and clothes, which they left in my care. Three times they went to the city and brought food and clothes and blankets. Where were you then, Ghorbati?"

The headman came in and sat next to Uncle Hosayn Ali. Uncle Hosayn Ali packed his chibouk and gave it to the headman. The headman puffed three times and asked Uncle Hosayn Ali, "Did you see Madam?"

Uncle Hosayn Ali said, "I didn't recognize her at first. She's really aged quite a bit."

The headman said, "It's been a year or so since their son died."

Uncle Hosayn Ali said, "I know. I paid them a visit on my way back from Mashhad."

Uncle Hosayn Ali told the story of Madam's only son— how he had contracted an illness that none of the doctors knew how to cure. Then he told of Madam's husband, who took the poor child to faraway places, from city to city, showing the boy to doctors everywhere, but the doctors were powerless to cure him. Then he went to dervishes and faith healers, but they turned the child away, and he died in some far-off land. Uncle Hosayn Ali said that Madam kept the child's room exactly as it was. She hadn't moved a thing in the room . . .

That night I'd paid the second installment on my goat and had thrown some onion, potato, carrot, and eggplant skins in front of him. The blue-eyed bearded guy promised to bring my goat a bell from Qazvin. The little thing had gotten so cute—when he was busy chewing cud, he'd follow me with his eyes, and when I came back from the hilltop, the little devil would jump and cavort, and when I took him around, he'd walk in step with me most of the way. He wouldn't get too far ahead of me and tire me out. I'd bring him water from Dr. Dana'ifard Ebrahimabadi's deep well. Besides, he had taken to my brother even more strongly than to me. Naneh Tajmah had said when she had a chance she'd spread henna over my goat's white forehead and legs, but I'd have to pay for the henna myself.

The next day on the hill it suddenly struck me—What if the old woman has designs on me? She came and sat beside me first thing and said, "Here, let me help you." She picked up the potshards herself, looking them over and putting them within the marked lines on the ground. She said, "I hear you don't have anyone except a brother?" I said, "Not quite, I also have a goat." She asked, "Would you like to come to Tehran?" I did, but I didn't reply. Ramazan, sitting next to me, said, "I've been to Tehran. My father's in jail in Tehran. I go to see him once a week."

Madam asked, "Why is your father in jail?"

Ramazan said, "They say he committed murder, but my father is innocent. This Ghorbati fellow was in cahoots with the headman and they gave false testimony."

Madam turned to me and said, "Khorrang, get up! Let's go to Graveyard Hill." I didn't make a move.

Ramazan stood up and said, "Madam, I'll come with you. Take me to Tehran and make me your servant." Madam ignored him. She started walking alone, and I saw her stoop, as though she bore a heavy load on her shoulders, and I felt sorry for her. I followed her and walked at her side. She took my hand and said, "I'll take you to Tehran and put you in school."

I pulled my hand back and said, "I'm not supposed to be on familiar terms with you, Madam." Madam laughed. I asked, "Are there jinn in Tehran?"

Madam laughed again and said, "Are there ever! They're all the brood of jinn." When Madam laughed, everyone was happy. It suddenly hit me that I was happy too. She asked, "What would you like?"

I said, "I'd like for my brother's leg to heal so he can come to the mounds, so he can go to school in Bu'in Zahra."

She said, "No, what do you wish for yourself?"

"What do you mean?" I asked.

She said, "For example, what would you like to do when you grow up?"

I said, "I want to be like the blue-eyed bearded guy."

We reached Graveyard Hill. They'd unearthed the skeleton of a dead man from I don't know how many thousands of years ago, and there was red clay scattered on it. They'd laid down the skeleton straight on the ground. The short, bearded gentleman's job now was to find the missing bones and stick them flush together. The village kids had given the short gentleman the name Mr. Bonesman. He stood up when Madam approached, but his eyes were on the skeleton. Then he picked up a deep stone jar full of red dust and a long, thin piece of stone, like a mortar and pestle, and showed it to Madam, saying, "It's red ocher. It was lying by the dead man's head."

Madam said, "This is Khorrang. He wants to become an archaeologist."

Mr. Bonesman said, "In Baramuh?" This guy knew the real name of our village.

Madam said, "No, he's coming with me to Tehran."

Mr. Bonesman replied, "He's in luck." Sitting by the skeleton, Madam took a handkerchief out of her purse and wiped the sweat off her face and the front and back of her neck. Her face had turned red, and her henna-tinted and white hair had stuck together. She took a look at Graveyard Hill and the bones of the dead, and said, "It's the morning of Resurrection. The dead have come out of their graves . . . " She thought for a moment and said again, "And hell is right here. Let's ask them to give account of themselves. We'll try to understand what they've accomplished and where they've gone with their lives." Mr. Bonesman asked, "Are you unwell this morning?"

Madam replied, "Oh no, I'm fine."

What she'd said was outright blasphemy, and I began to worry for her.

We went back. We stood under a withered tree, abandoned in the wilderness, under the sun. Ali Asghar, middleman for the Americans, was coming toward us, holding a large nylon bag in his hand. He kept walking until he reached us. He stopped in front of Madam, took off his hat, and greeted her. He said, "Madam, I'd like to speak with you." Other than the three of us and the sun and that withered tree, there was nothing and no one else in the wilderness, and I knew he'd come to take Madam's life, because she'd blasphemed. He was more than a match for me and Madam. He was big and wore a dust-stained dark blue jacket and trousers. Madam said, "What do you want?" Ali Asghar said, "Please ask the doctor to set me up with some work." He got very close to Madam. I shouted, "Ali Asghar, I'll report you to the headman. Go on, get out of here." I bent down and picked up a rock to throw at him. Madam grabbed my hand and said, "Are you out of your mind, boy?" She turned to Ali Asghar and asked, "What were you doing before?" Ali Asghar said, "I bought manuscripts and antiques and sold them to Mr. Rabi in Tehran. Now I can't earn my bread."

I said, "What the hell does anyone care that you can't earn your bread?"

Ali Asghar said, "You used to be my own customer, boy . . ."

And he got closer to Madam and took her hand. I yelled, "Take your hand off another person's wife!" He kissed Madam's hand and I hit him—I was pounding him with my fists. Madam said, "Khorrang, you've gone crazy!" She pulled me off Ali Asghar and said to him, "Very well, I'll commend you to the doctor." Ali Asghar bowed his head like a lamb and walked away.

We started out for Sakezabad Hill and the wind was chasing us from behind. Madam asked, "What did you hit the fellow for?" I said, "I thought he was going to take your life." "Why would he take my life?" she asked. "You blasphemed," I said. "Now there'll either be an earthquake or . . . " She laughed and asked, "Who is this Ali Asghar that you dislike him so much?" I said, "He'd come to buy the village women's hair and pack it up and send it to America. But the village women didn't sell. How can a woman cut her hair and give it to a strange man and have it fall into the hands of unclean Westerners?"

Madam said, "The village women did well. Hair is part of one's body."

They built a little one-room mud hut for the watchman and made Ali Asghar guard over the potshards and bones of the dead. It was agreed that every night one of us would take turns watching with him; we'd also take along the big black village dog. The third night it was my turn. We sat down and I stared at the dark wilderness, while Ali Asghar griped about my hitting him, but I didn't answer. Then he said, "If Madam wasn't going to make you her servant, I'd settle your hash this very night . . . " and he stretched out and slept soundly. The village dog, too, laid its head on its paws and slept. Suddenly I missed my brother. It was pitch dark. I was struck by fear of the risen dead and the Day of Resurrection—which Madam had said would come any day now—and Ali Asghar. This was perhaps the first time in my life that I was afraid. I got up, moved the pillow to my place, and drew the blanket over it. Ali Asghar rolled over and said, "Hey." I waited a little, and when he didn't say anything more, I bolted and ran all the way to the coffeehouse. My heart was beating so hard I could hear it. My brother was asleep. I put my arms around him and lay down and relaxed.

I heard him say in his sleep, "Khorrang, Khorrang!" So I told him, "I'm here, brother." My brother put his hand on my back. Then I turned and put my head on his breastbone.

I had next morning off, but I went to the mound to see what was up. The blue-eyed bearded guy was grilling Ali Asghar. Madam saw me and shook her head. Farajollah had laid aside his shovel and was listening to their conversation. Ali Asghar was saying, "My dear sir, I was awake. I just thought it was a jinni, so I didn't answer. You know, the jinn take your shape and call to me." The blue-eyed bearded guy laughed and asked, "What does a jinni look like?" Farajollah butted in: "It's got hooves and an eye in its forehead." The blue-eyed bearded guy's eyes fell on me and he asked, "Khorrang, where were you?" I said, "Sir, last night the jinn had a wedding and I went to watch." Farajollah said, "Doctor, he's telling the truth. I went to their wedding too. They were jumping here and jumping there." The blue-eyed bearded guy laughed, his white teeth flashing in the sun, and he asked, "What about the dog? Why didn't the dog bark?"

Farajollah said, "My dear sir, dogs are afraid of jinn. The poor dog has spent so much time sleeping and not being able to catch jinn that he's gotten thin. A dog should wander freely and get bones from the butcher shop, not eat only bread and pretend to be asleep for fear of jinn."

Madam put a hand on my shoulder and said, "Khorrang, let's go. Show me the village. It's cooler today."

Farajollah said, "This morning the Miyeh started up."

I didn't want to go with Madam. She was touching me all over, completely careless of what was lawful and what wasn't. I said, "I wasn't on watch last night. I went to the coffeehouse and slept there."

Madam said, "Excellent. Always tell the truth."

We started off for Uncle Hosayn Ali's farm. Madam's word was law. Madam took my hand and this time I didn't pull back. She asked, "Would you like to come to Tehran and be my son?"

I said, "Respected Madam, I'm not your son."

She said, "I'd like to adopt you as my child."

I said, "Dear lady, what'll happen to my brother and my goat?"

She said, "You'll give your goat to your brother and, whenever you want, you'll come and pay your brother a visit. It's not too far."

I said, "Dear lady, can't you adopt both my brother and me as your children?"

She said, "No, I don't want two sons. Besides, your brother is grown."

I don't know what came over me, but I pulled my hand away from Madam's and stopped. I said, "Yes, Madam. My brother is a cripple. Besides, you don't want a child. As Ali Asghar says, you want a servant. Yes, after all Your Excellency's servant has to be healthy and not tell lies." And I cried.

Madam wiped away my tears with her hands and held my head against her. She said, "No, my dear, I don't want a servant. I want a child, I give you my word. I've stayed in the village these past few days for your sake. We'll put it all on paper with your brother and the headman." I was still crying, as though the earthquake had happened just yesterday and I had lost mama and papa. Madam kissed my hair and said, "Don't cry, little lizard." I was no lizard, but it felt like she'd said, "Hush." I'd liked it that she'd wiped away my tears and held my head against her and kissed my hair and called me "little lizard." I neither cried any more, nor did I say another word, and I kept my head where it was. Madam smelled of apples.

We started off again. Madam said, "At first you'll have a bad time in Tehran, but after you've been there awhile, you'll get used to it. I'll try to make it easier for you so it won't be so bad." Well, I wanted to go to Tehran to see what it was like. It didn't matter whether I was adopted by Madam or not. I was nobody's child. I was a scrawny cat sitting at Kablai Asadollah's table or Uncle Hosayn Ali's . . . and if I saw this was leading to my being a servant, I'd run away and come back to the village. After all, I wasn't going to be outdone by Ramazan.

Ramazan used to say, "Tehran is really something to see. Imagine our village a thousand times—that's what Tehran is like. The streets there are much wider than Ebrahimabad's

Vali-Ahd Street. The potholes are also bigger than the pot-holes of Vali-Ahd Street. There's no grass anywhere, either. The evil eye is on all the trees there, but they have more policemen than you could ever want. The police are almost always everywhere. It's lit up every night too."

We reached Uncle Hosayn Ali's farm. The plots were covered with water, sewage water, and the smell of water and dust was in the air. The Miyeh breeze was cooling. As soon as Uncle Hosayn Ali saw us, he buttoned his vest and untied the handkerchief from his chin. I guess he had a toothache. He came toward us, greeted Madam, and said, "Welcome." He took the lady to the arbor made of rushes in the middle of the field and shouted, "Morvarid, Golab-tun, hey!" Then he himself ran in the direction of the vineyard. I really wanted to run after him and see his scare-crow for this year.

Morvarid came out of the vineyard with a bunch of dark grapes in her hand. She'd put on a thin *chador*. Because of me she'd covered her face, but her hair showed. Like her sister, Golabtun had also put on a *chador*, but she hadn't covered her face. Both of them were like grown-up ladies. They came into the arbor and Morvarid offered Madam grapes. Madam took a single grape and asked both of them how they were. She said, "Give Khorrang some, too." Mor-varid held the grapes in front of me and I also plucked a single one and put it in my mouth. It was covered with dust.

Madam said, "Khorrang, take more." I was feeling anxious. Like the mound, I'd become unstable.

Uncle Hosayn Ali brought a pillow, put it on the ground in the arbor, and said to Madam, "Please sit down." Madam sat on the pillow and Uncle Hosayn Ali sat on the ground facing her. Morvarid and Golabtun also sat down.

Madam said, "It's a pretty farm you have, pretty children too."

Uncle Hosayn Ali said, "They're at your service."

Madam said, "Your village produces onions, potatoes, and pretty children."

Uncle Hosayn Ali said, "If the Jews would only let us. They've sunk deep wells and dried up our aqueducts."

Madam said, "I hear their agriculture didn't take off."

Uncle Hosayn Ali replied, "They forgot the winds here. They'd have done better to plant pistachios."

Madam said, "So they made no improvements for you."

Uncle Hosayn Ali replied, "Well, they taught us cleft grafting. They planted several apple orchards too. They're growing a little bit here, a little bit there."

I don't know why their talk made me so restless. I wanted to go to the vineyard and eat my fill of grapes.

Uncle Hosayn Ali's wife brought Madam tea and said hello and sat down. Madam herself poured everyone tea—modesty was not a part of her character. She talked to all of them as she would to her own kin. But my attention was focused on Morvarid and Golabtun. Uncle Hosayn Ali's wife spoke to them in the Tati dialect, but I understood. She told them to go pick some grapes for Madam and to wash the grapes in water from the jug. The girls got up and left.

Madam turned to Uncle Hosayn Ali and his wife, saying, "I want to adopt Khorrang as my child."

Uncle Hosayn Ali said, "You'll be blessed for it."

Uncle Hosayn Ali's wife turned to me and said, "How lucky you are, boy, that such a lady has found you." If I was adopted by Madam, she'd definitely give her daughters to my brother and me.

Morvarid came back with a tray full of large red grapes, shining like lamps, and put the tray in front of Madam. Golabtun also came in, and they both sat down. Madam talked with them and asked what class they were in and what their teacher was like. Then she asked Uncle Hosayn Ali for the addresses of the Bu'in Zahra shops and bathhouse and barbershop and what roads they took and whether people bought National shoes. Then she told Uncle Hosayn Ali she'd see him that evening in the coffeehouse and she also wanted to see the headman. Good God, what a busybody and chatterbox she was, either eating grapes or asking questions!

We walked along to the coffeehouse and my brother brought Madam tea. Madam was sitting on the cot on Naneh Tajmah's handwoven rug. I sat next to her. Now if she put her hand on my head I wouldn't knock it away. She stroked the pile of the rug and caressed it and told my brother that she wanted to adopt me as her child. My brother burst into tears. How he cried and cried! Madam said, "My dear boy, you should be happy. It's not that far. He'll always be your brother—he's not going to disown his relationship with you. Besides, whenever you miss him, you can come see him."

My brother wiped his eyes and said, "I can't just leave the coffeehouse . . . how am I going to come to Tehran with this leg?"

Madam said, "He himself has agreed, but if you don't agree, I won't take him."

I said, "Brother, give your permission. I really want to go to Tehran and see what it's like."

My brother said, "They're going to start up the seventh and eighth grades here. They're going to pave Vali-Ahd Street. The Tourist Office has agreed to give money to Kablai Asadollah to whitewash the coffeehouse and put up pictures of the Shah and the Crown Prince and the Imam Ali on the walls. We're buying a radio for the coffeehouse. I've heard they're going to bring in an expert from Tehran to teach the village women and children real rug-weaving. The flower designs on the rugs will be done according to pattern. We're supposed to weave carpets for export. I'm thinking myself of doing rug-weaving in the mornings and working in the coffeehouse afternoons and nights."

I said, "Brother, take me rug-weaving with you."

My brother said, "No, you go and become this lady's son. Become a servant in other people's houses."

I said, "She doesn't want me as a servant, she wants me as her child. Isn't that right, Madam?"

Madam said, "How many times do I have to say it? It doesn't seem to sink in." Madam was upset.

My brother said, "They're also going to bring telephones and electricity here. Everyone will get a telephone and electricity. I've heard they're going to fix up the caravanserai at Mohammadabad Khorreh and make it a center of learning, and all the scholars will come to the caravanserai and give each other lessons. We have a literacy corps and rural development corps, too."

Madam said, "Do you really have a literacy corps and rural development corps?"

My brother said, "We've had them for some time. If you want, I can show you where they are—right by the doctor's garden."

With my brother limping in front and Madam and me following behind, we went to the doctor's garden and showed Madam the signs for the corps. Madam asked, "Are they set up in the garden?"

I laughed and said, "No, this garden belongs to Dr. Dana'ifard Ebrahimabadi."

My brother snapped, "Shut up, kid."

Madam asked, "So where are the corps set up?"

My brother said, "Right here."

Madam replied, "I mean, where are the people?"

My brother said, "The people haven't come yet. They're coming later."

Toward late afternoon, Madam sat behind the wheel of the marked car, just like a man. I sat by her elbow as she started out. I don't know why, but I'd suddenly become very fainthearted. I was afraid she'd upend the car. I was afraid she'd slam the car into the Jews' trees. But we drove to Bu'in Zahra with no trouble. Now I was afraid she wouldn't be able to stop the car and it would go on and on until it ran out of gas and we'd be lost. But Madam took a look around and stopped the car in front of Ali Akbar's shop. We went in and she bought me two pairs of socks, two undershirts and underpants, a pair of blue trousers like the blue-eyed bearded guy's, and a blue shirt. She said, "Put these on." But I was embarrassed to undress in front of her. So she took a rough measurement from my worsted jacket and black twill trousers, meaning she held up the shirt in front of me and gave me the trousers, telling me to hold them in front of my legs. Then she stepped back a little, squinted her eyes, and looked at me. She also bought a little brown trunk and arranged the clothes in it so neatly that, with one look, you could tell where the pants and shirts were. Then we went to the National shoe store. I sat in front of the mirror while the store owner kept putting shoes on my feet and taking them off. Other than rubber shoes, I'd never had shoes on my feet before in my life. Most of the shoes were either too tight or too wide—or Madam didn't like them. What a difficult thing it was to buy shoes! Finally she liked a pair and asked me, "Are they tight?" They were, but I was so tired I didn't let on.

She left me in the hands of the bath attendant and said, "Wash him thoroughly." Then she said, "Khorrang, I'll wait for you in the car. If you're late, come to the coffee-house across the street." She went everywhere so easily. Our women never went into a coffeehouse.

I came out from the bath and put on my new clothes. She'd told me to throw away my worsted jacket and black pants, but I hid them both under my new clothes.

Freshly scrubbed and clean and dressed in my new clothes, I sat beside Madam. But I wasn't myself anymore; I had turned into another Khorrang. I had a nice deep sleep before we reached Ebrahimabad, waking up only a few times: once when Madam stopped the car and I raised my head to see the headman's donkeys, laden with potatoes and onions, passing by; the second time when Madam brushed my hair off my forehead; and finally when Madam gently scratched my hand and it felt good and I heard her say, "My dear, we've arrived."

We were at the Baramuh coffeehouse, and the sun still hadn't set. Madam honked and both of us got out of the car. I put my hand in Madam's and she took it and squeezed it gently. When my brother saw me, he said, "Khorrang, you've become like a gentleman's son." And he sat on the coffeehouse counter, rubbing his knee. Madam came into the coffeehouse, and little by little all the village folk gathered in the coffeehouse to gawk at Madam. Naneh Tajmah dashed home and came back with her hand full. She said a prayer and blew at me and moved her clenched fist in circles over my head and Madam's, and tossed what she had brought into the fire. Then she whispered in my ear, "Tell Madam to buy a rug from me." She undid her prayer *chador* from her waist and put it on.

My brother brought Madam tea. Uncle Hosayn Ali and the headman also arrived and sat on the same cot as Madam. Farajollah and the kids from our village came in from the mounds. The womenfolk and other children had also turned out in droves. My brother pumped the coffeehouse gas lamp, but there was a hitch in the works somewhere and it wouldn't start up. Madam turned to the headman and said aloud, so everyone would hear, "I want to adopt Khorrang as my child." The headman said, "I heard from Uncle Hosayn Ali." Ramazan had come up to me. He

felt my pants with his hands. The other kids came up too.
They bent down to look at my shoes. Ramazan whispered
in my ear, "Tell her to adopt me, too. Then I can go see my
father every day." Naneh Tajmah said, "Praise God! Lord,
how your majesty becomes you. You raised this child out of
the ashes." Madam said to her, "Please sit." And she sat next
to Madam. Again my brother burst into tears and Uncle
Hosayn Ali said, "Mohsen, don't cry. He's going to a fine
city. He'll become a mullah in the capital. It'll be good for
you, too." Farajollah said, "It'll be good for all of us." As for
me, I wanted to take my shoes off—they were pinching.
And then I wanted to tell the story of the two pigeons, one
of whom flew away.

At sundown, Madam and the old man with bright eyes and I
piled into the marked car to drive to Tehran. All the village
folk had come to say good-bye. Naneh Tajmah had brought
a Koran and we passed under it to ensure a safe journey.
Uncle Hosayn Ali, his wife and daughters, the headman, all
the folks from the mounds, Farajollah, Ali Asghar, and my
brother were all crowded around the car. Golabtun was
looking at me as if we had gotten engaged. Everyone was
looking at me. Uncle Hosayn Ali gave me a handkerchief full
of grapes. I threw my arms around my brother and he began
to sob bitterly. I said, "Brother, don't cry. I'll go to Tehran

and become a doctor and come back to cure your leg." Now, for my brother's sake, I was prepared to become a doctor and not be like the blue-eyed bearded guy. My brother had brought my goat to the car and I badly wanted Madam to let me put my goat in the car too and take him to Tehran. But Ramazan had said there wasn't any grass in Tehran, and I was afraid my goat would starve without grass. When I got in, Farajollah whispered to me, "When I come to Tehran, I'll come straight to Mr. Khorrang's house and I'll teach you what to do and what not to do."

The old man drove, with Madam sitting at his side. I sat behind them and the brown trunk was next to me and the handkerchief with the grapes was on top. As we left the village I started to cry, suddenly remembering that my shoes were tight and were pinching, and I began to miss my brother, my goat, and Golabtun. I lowered my head on my arm and cried. Madam ran her hand back and forth through my hair, saying, "Don't cry, my dear, you'll adjust." But this time I knocked her hand away. The old man asked Madam, "Is this the right thing to do?" Madam said, "I don't know." I told myself the story of the two pigeons and cried even harder.

When we reached the caravanserai at Mohammadabad Khorreh, the car stopped and the old man and Madam got out and went inside. When they were out of sight, the urge hit me. First I took off my shoes, then my shirt and pants. I pulled out my worsted jacket and my black twill trousers from under the new clothes in the trunk and put them on. I got out of the car and hid behind a tree. My heart was thumping in my ears, as though someone was pounding drums. The same gendarme who had put the handcuffs on Ramazan's father approached until he came right up to me. Suddenly he shouted, "What have you come here for, boy?" He reached to grab me by the scruff of the neck when Madam shouted from the roof of the caravanserai, "Leave him alone!" My eyes met Madam's. Now I didn't know whether to go back and get in the car or run away to our village. From her perch Madam asked, "Why barefoot, you stupid boy? At least put on your shoes." Then I took off. The gendarme yelled, "Madam, should I catch him?" "No, let him go," Madam said. "To hell with him." I ran and ran. Thorns stuck in my feet and it was getting dark and I was scared. I, who had never been afraid of any jinni or corpse or hill, was now filled with fear. I imagined that the same dead man whose bones Mr. Bonesman had found and stuck flush together was chasing me with long strides, his skull rattling on his backbone.

I imagined that the bones of the dead had begun to move and were running behind the skeleton and were catching up to me to strangle me. I imagined that in every ditch and at the foot of every tree there was a mass of jinn sitting and having weddings and funerals and circumcision ceremonies and everything. I imagined snakes and dragons were lying in wait to sting my bare feet. I imagined that my brother, missing me, had wandered into the wilderness, and was coming after me, limping and hobbling. If only he'd catch up. There wasn't a sound in the wilderness, but I could hear the hooting and laughter and weeping of the jinn underground. And under the dome of the sky, the air carried the voices of the spirits of the dead, whispering and jabbering and deafening me.

Exhausted, I sat under one of the Jews' apple trees, picked an apple to eat, and waited for the bus. But could I be calm? I imagined the gendarme and the old man and Madam had gotten in their marked car and were coming to run me over out of spite. I heard footsteps and human voices. I hid behind the tree and craned my neck. Farajollah and Ali Asghar the middleman were coming, each with a saddlebag in his hand. Oh, so these two had chanced on the treasure. These two had found the royal jar, and the gold and jewels were in the saddlebags.

I heard the bus and I stepped into the road and flagged it down. The bus stopped and I got on. I didn't have any money, either, and my socks were full of thorns and nettles. But lo and behold! Madam was sitting in the bus, too. I wanted to run away, but the bus had started moving. Madam cleared a place for me to sit next to her, but I went and sat in the back of the bus.

We reached Baramuh and everyone got off, except me and Madam. Madam was standing by the third row of seats and I was sitting in the back. Madam said, "You stupid boy, if you didn't want to come with us, why didn't you say so? Now I have to hand you back to your brother and get back my papers." My brother's hand had shaken as he signed that paper. I hoped to God he hadn't set off into the wilderness out of grief.

I let Madam take me by the hand and we got off. All the folks gathered at the coffeehouse door. My brother came limping and threw his arms around me and kissed me. Naneh Tajmah brought candy nuggets and sugarplums and scattered them over my head. Madam and the headman went inside the coffeehouse.

Then the old man arrived in the marked car. Madam took the trunk and the handkerchief full of grapes from the car and put them on the ground. She didn't put them in my hands. Madam got in the car and turned to me and smiled, but there were tears in her eyes. She seemed so old. It seemed she'd aged a thousand years.

# A City Like Paradise

Every night, the Negro girl Mehrangiz came to sleep in the children's room. The bedrolls were spread in the large room, one beside the other. Ali and his two sisters lay down in the dust they had raised from the carpet and the mattresses with their play. The bedroll at the end, the most ragged, belonged to Mehrangiz. Every night it was the same. The older sister lowered the wick in the oil lamp, waiting for Mehrangiz to come to bed. Mehrangiz washed the dishes in the kitchen across from the room, and Ali could hear the dishes clanking and the water splattering.

When Mehrangiz turned out the light in the kitchen, Ali bunched himself up in the bed with excitement, pressing his face into the pillow. Mehrangiz blew out the lamp with one breath and lay down in bed so quietly that, had Ali not lain awake, he would never have known. Then Ali would call to Mehrangiz, pleading for stories. And every night, the same stories were repeated—the stories of Mehrangiz and her mother and other Negresses.

In one story, Mehrangiz's mother is a child, playing by the river with the other black children, stark naked, when a man wearing a kaffiyeh and headband dismounts from the camel litter and shouts in Arabic, "Come! Come!" Only Mehrangiz's mother runs to him. The ugly fellow gives her a handful of large sugared almonds, picks her up and puts her in the litter. Mehrangiz's mother, then a very young child, cries and struggles. A hand clamps down over her mouth, and she bites the hand. The hand smacks her hard on the mouth and she bleeds. She cries so much that she falls asleep with exhaustion. Upon waking, she finds herself on a ship. Many Negroes—men, women, and children—are aboard, but her mother is not there, nor her father. Again she cries and cries and cries. A black woman puts a red apple in her hand. Mehrangiz's mother asks innocently, "Are we going to my mama?" The woman raps herself on the back of the hand, shakes her head and says, "O woe! O unhappy day!" in their own language. (Mehrangiz's mother still remembers this language, but Mehrangiz doesn't know it.) Then they sell Mehrangiz's mother to Ali's grandfather, who names her Baji Delnavaz.

Ali had heard this story many times, and every night when he heard it again he swore that if he got his hands on the strange man he'd cut him into pieces with the kitchen knife. Mehrangiz would say, "All right, go to sleep now."

Another night, the story would go like this: Nur ol-Saba, the Navvabs' Negress, excelled over all the others. First of all, she wasn't as tawny as Mehrangiz and her mother. Her nose wasn't broad, but narrow. Her eyes, too, weren't round, but almond-shaped, and her hair wasn't frizzy—just like the two statuettes of the Negresses that stood by the clock in the reception room.

"Not like me, sweetheart, who's got no eyebrows at all, and eyes like split peas, and a nose flat as a straw mat, and lips like sticks. I was still in your grandfather's house, sweetheart, when she came one day from the Navvabs' house to your grandfather's house. She'd come to invite the ladies to the mourning service for Mr. Navvab. They'd shot Mr. Navvab in front of the consulate. She was wearing a black crêpe de Chine *chador*. When she walked in the door, she bent her head ever so slightly so she wouldn't bump the doorpost—she was that tall. She didn't kiss your grandmother's shoulder, either. All she said was, 'Hello.' That was all. She took a saucer of coffee beans from a black silk handkerchief and put it in front of your grandmother . . .

"Then word spread in all of Shiraz who and what Nur ol-Saba was. One day, sweetheart, three brand new carriages pull up in front of Mr. Navvab's garden. One black man in a suit and fur hat gets down from the first carriage, then other blacks after him, all in fur hats and bow ties and neckties. Last of all comes a black with a trunk in his hand, covered in red velvet. Sweetheart, these were all ministers and big shots from Nur ol-Saba's city. They knock on the door and come into Navvab's house. Navvab's wife sends for Nur ol-Saba. When Nur ol-Saba comes, all of them bow to her. And they bow to her over and over. In the trunk, sweetheart, there are silk dresses and lots of jewels. They give them to Nur ol-Saba and she puts them on. As she's walking past to get into the carriage, the blacks bow again. They're bowing to her so low their heads touch their knees. Now she must be the queen of her city. From that day on, sweetheart, it's every black's dream in Shiraz for someone to come and take them away."

And Ali would say, "Maybe they'll come for you too. If they come, Mammy, will you leave me and go?"

Mehrangiz would say, "Now go to sleep. We'll see in the morning."

That was how Ali knew that Mehrangiz's mother was Baji Delnavaz. But what about her father? Ali's mother often spoke of her own father's slaves, of the meals where they had seated twenty people at a time. She'd recall her mother's voyage to Mecca and her father's jokes with the skipper. She hadn't seen any of it, of course, only heard about it.

Ali's mother would say Baji Delnavaz had been the favorite of the slaves. They'd even taken her on the pilgrimage to Mecca. But she'd become capricious after the voyage. The things she'd done! Mehrangiz, too, had been a playmate to children of gentility. Mother would fret about how she was forced to put Mehrangiz to work in her husband's house: "One doesn't put the prize of her trousseau to work. The prize of the trousseau keeps the lady's strongbox. But where's the strongbox for Mehrangiz to keep?"

Ali even remembered the day when Baji Delnavaz came to their house, leaning on a cane and looking like a tree festooned with rags. Mother was washing at the pool for prayer. As she wiped her feet she called, "Come, Mehrangiz. Your mother's here." Mehrangiz flung herself out of the kitchen and threw her arms around her mother.

Ali's mother stood for prayer. Ali and his sisters were gathered in the parlor, their reception room, and sat quietly with their legs folded, unlike usual. Baji Delnavaz sat at the end of the room near the door. Weeping, she told them that her master had thrown her out in her old age. Now she had no place to go. Ali and his younger sister started to cry. But the older sister said, "Let's go play." The younger sister brought her old jacket and gave it to Delnavaz. Ali liked that. So he brought all the goodies he had hidden away and spread them in Delnavaz's lap. Mother continued praying, sometimes raising the level of her voice. Despite his age, Ali knew she was remonstrating with them; he even knew that she had deliberately prolonged her prayer. She sat in prayer so long that Ali lost patience. Finally, Mother struck her knees three times and Ali breathed more easily. Delnavaz came and kissed mother's shoulder. She was stammering. She began to retell her story from the beginning: "If Master was alive, I wouldn't be in this state." Ali's mother said, "I heard it all. That'll do." Delnavaz said, "Please let me sleep in the coal bin tonight." Mother said, "That I can't do. How many mouths must we feed? As it is, with Mehrangiz we have more than we can deal with." Delnavaz said, "I'll have to go begging. I'm an invalid." Ali's mother said, "What do I care? Go ahead." Ali and his younger sister burst into tears, pleading with Mother to keep Delnavaz. Mother glared at them.

Then they heard the click-clack of Delnavaz's cane from the corridor. They had opened the shutters in the parlor and Ali was sitting on the sill, nagging and pleading with Mother. Mother said, "Get up, boy." Then she yelled, "Delnavaz, go to Monavvar Khanom's house. Is it my fault that I'm the older sister?"

Ali went to Mehrangiz in the kitchen. Mehrangiz was putting firewood in the oven as Ali sat beside her. Tears flowed down her face. One teardrop slid down her chin and onto her neck. Ali said, "Don't cry, Mammy. If Auntie doesn't take her in, when I grow up myself, I'll . . . "

Mehrangiz said, "I wasn't crying. I got smoke in my eyes."

Ali said, "What smoke?"

Mehrangiz put a finger to her nose and said, "Don't tell Madam I was crying, all right?"

A month passed, perhaps even less. Late one afternoon, Monavvar Khanom's husband came looking for Mehrangiz. She'd gone to the public bath. Monavvar Khanom's husband was whispering in Mother's ear and she was shaking her head and saying, "Good Lord! What a bother for my poor sister." Then Mother got up and said, "Ali, run quickly to the bath. Tell Mehrangiz to come at once." As Ali was putting on his shoes, he heard Mother's voice as she said to Monavvar Khanom's husband, "Why don't you go with him? I don't want her to come here yammering and blubbering. Just take her along with you."

Ali and his uncle reached the bath and stood behind the canvas screen. Ali's uncle called the bath attendant and said something to her quietly. The attendant walked away while they waited behind the screen. Ali heard Mehrangiz saying, "Give me time to wash my blasted hair and I'll come." A woman's voice answered, "Can't be. It's urgent. Hurry."

Again Mehrangiz's voice said, "Has someone come for my hand, Mistress?" And they heard the snapping of fingers. The woman's voice said, "Your mother's in her death throes and you snap your fingers?"

A scream, and Ali started to cry.

All three started walking. Mehrangiz fell down in the street three times. They walked into Monavvar Khanom's house.

Monavvar Khanom asked her husband, "What have you brought the child for?"

"He came himself."

His aunt yelled, "Nayyer, come. Ali's here." She turned to her husband and said, "God rest her soul! She died at an evil hour. It's twilight."

Nayyer and Ali went to play. She said, "Ali, come let's play dead."

Ali asked, "Is Baji Delnavaz dead?"

Nayyer said, "Yes, they're going to take her to the bath."

Forty days after the death of Delnavaz, Ali and Mehrangiz went to her gravesite in Saffeh-ye Torbat. They searched a great deal and asked many people before they found her grave. It was a mound of earth with a brick laid on top. Mehrangiz hugged the mound and wept so bitterly that Ali was frightened.

That night, Ali was waiting for Mehrangiz to put out the light in the kitchen and come and tell stories. A new story had been added to Mehrangiz's store now, that of her mother's death. But there was no sign of Mehrangiz. The light in the kitchen went out and Mehrangiz still did not come. Ali was anxious and could not sleep. It was very late when he heard Mehrangiz whispering and then saw his father's shadow pass the room.

Next morning Father had lost his glasses. They searched everywhere. Even the children were looking. But Mother did not seem in the least bit bothered that Aqa's glasses were lost, and did not help. She was even snickering. Ali did not like that snicker. He went to his mother's prayer rug—perhaps he'd find the glasses in the folds of the rug. No sooner had he begun to push away the folds than Mother grabbed and flung him to the middle of the room. "You're defiling it!" she screamed. In the end, Father went to work without his glasses. But after that night he always went to bed with his glasses on.

Ali was not going to school yet, but his two sisters were. One day, he saw something terrible. Mehrangiz had accompanied the children to school and come back. Ali's mother was in the kitchen. Ali was sitting at the window in the children's room and could see everything that happened. When Mehrangiz entered the kitchen, Ali's mother clubbed her over the head with a piece of wood. Ali jumped down from his perch into the courtyard. He ran into the kitchen and tried to restrain his mother's hand. He was crying. But Mother was snickering. Mehrangiz's head was bruised and bleeding. Ali said, weeping, "Don't hit her. I'm scared, I'm scared." But Mehrangiz was not crying. Mother said, "It's the nigger who's bleeding. What's the matter with you?" Mehrangiz went and sat down by the pool and washed her head. The bleeding did not stop, though, and Ali was wonder-struck that she wasn't crying. Mother picked up the waterpipe burner that stood by the pool and poured tobacco ash into the wound. She said, "You'll become a whore yet." Ali kept asking, "What's a whore?" Mother said, "I'll get a midwife." Ali said, "Housewife?" Mehrangiz burst into tears.

The unfortunate thing about summer was that Ali and Mehrangiz would be separated. They'd set up the beds over the pool and Mother and Father and the children would sleep there. Mehrangiz would sleep on the ground in the middle of the courtyard.

One day at sundown Monavvar Khanom and her daughter came visiting. Monavvar Khanom sat cross-legged on the bed beside Ali's mother. The waterpipe spout was between her lips and she was saying something very softly and crying, wiping away the tears with a corner of her scarf. The children were playing capture-the-fort on the steps that led to the parlor. Nayyer and Ali were on one side and the rest of the children on the other. Once when Nayyer and Ali stormed the fort and took it, they hugged and kissed each other. Watching the children while listening to her sister's woes, Ali's mother yelled at him, "Shame on you, boy!" Monavvar Khanom laid aside her waterpipe and said, "What's wrong with it, sister? Haven't we raised them for each other?" Mother said, "We'll have to see what fate ordains."

Monavvar Khanom and her daughter stayed that night and slept in the bed in Ali's father's place. After a good deal of arguing, Mehrangiz was told to pick up the washed dishes from the cot in the kitchen and put them on the shelf. They pulled the cot out of the kitchen and spread Aqa's bedding on it. Mother was insisting that Mehrangiz sleep in the room that night, but relented when Monavvar Khanom intervened: "She'll suffocate from the heat, sister."

The moon was out that night and Ali could not fall asleep because the moonlight was in his eyes. When he did nod off finally, he woke again with a start. He was anxious about his wet mattress being put out to dry next morning with his cousin watching. His mother usually did it with a great deal of vociferous reproach. Mother was asleep and Monavvar Khanom was snoring. Ali thought he could hear Mehrangiz whispering. He was overjoyed. He called, "Mammy, Mammy!" Then he sat up in bed. It seemed his father's quilt was swollen. He was reminded of the story of Bakhtak that Mehrangiz told. He was waiting for his father to grab Bakhtak's earthen nose and adjure him to show him where the treasure was hidden. But he couldn't see Bakhtak's nose, and Bakhtak was moving and struggling. Ali was overcome by fear, but he was still hopeful. Finally, the swelling of the quilt went down and Bakhtak got up. Ali yelled, "Grab it. Grab his nose." Mother snapped, "Go to sleep." Ali wet himself.

Next morning it was the piece of wood again and Mehrangiz's bruised and bleeding head and Ali's wet mattress, which they'd laid upright against the wall. Mehrangiz looked at him sadly and said, "You shouldn't have done that."

Monavvar Khanom and Nayyer stayed a few days, until Ali's uncle came to their house. Monavvar Khanom hid in the back of the parlor. Then she came out and cried and they all left together. As they left, Ali's mother said aloud, "Don't forget to send her, sister."

A few days later a stout woman with red hair and henna-tinted arms and legs came to their house. Ali's mother stood to greet the woman, offered her the honored chair, and sat beside her. No matter how many times she called to Mehrangiz to bring refreshments, there was no answer. Mother sent Ali to fetch Mehrangiz. Mehrangiz was squatting on the kitchen cot, trembling like a willow. Ali asked, "What's the matter? Are you cold? Why don't you go into the sunlight?" But Mehrangiz wasn't budging, and although she heard Ali's mother, she did not answer. Finally the stout woman came into the kitchen. Standing with arms akimbo, she asked, "Well, are you coming or do I have to?" She dragged Mehrangiz kicking and screaming to the parlor and locked the door from the inside. Ali and his sisters were outside the door. Ali's older sister whispered something to the younger sister and they both chuckled.

Mehrangiz's screams rose from inside the room. Ali cried and mumbled, "Mammy, my Mammy!"

Ali was preparing for his high school exams when Father became an invalid. Father had nurtured many dreams, none of which had come to fruition. He wasn't even able to have electricity brought to the house. It had been a year that Monavvar Khanom's family had electricity. With Father's condition deteriorating, they found a suitor for Ali's younger sister; out of concern for the older sister, however, Father gave the suitor the cold shoulder.

On the night before the physics exam, Ali was laboring to grasp specific gravity when Mehrangiz entered the room in trepidation. Her eyes were round with terror and she was panting. She had become frail now. "What's the matter?" Ali asked. Mehrangiz said, "Aqa, there's an owl on the roof, laughing. I'm very scared. Owls know everything. They're prophets among the birds."

Ali asked, "What are you afraid of?"

"Aqa, your father . . . "

"Well, what do you suggest I do?" Ali asked.

Mehrangiz said, "Aqa, we have to adjure him."

Ali and Mehrangiz climbed the stairs to the roof. Mehrangiz held a tray with a Koran, green leaves, bread, and salt. She crossed the roof silently and sat behind the owl. Holding up the Koran, she murmured softly, "By this Koran, by this bread and salt . . . " Ali wanted to laugh. The owl spread its wings like a fan and flew away. Mehrangiz was relieved. She said, "He's gone. Now he'll go back to his ruins. He never builds nests, just lives in ruins. Good riddance."

Ali's father died the following week and Ali failed his exams. Now the breadwinner of the family, he did not go to school the next year. The accounting house where his father had worked hired him. At noon on the first day of work, Ali imitated his boss for Mehrangiz and his sisters. He dragged his cane on the floor, spat, opened the drawer with a key, poured tea into a matchbox and counted six sugar cubes and placed them on the table. Mehrangiz and the sisters were rolling with laughter. But Mother remonstrated: "Don't laugh. Your father is still not cold in the grave."

Hearing the words "father" and "grave," Mehrangiz went into the kitchen and bawled. Ali's mother yelled, "Mehrangiz, pick up your things and get out of this house. We don't need another mouth to feed." Mehrangiz bawled crazily, pounding herself in the head and pulling at her hair. Ali took her arm and led her to the pool and said, "Splash water on your face. As if I'd let you leave this house."

Toward late summer, at the insistence of Monavvar Khanom, Ali's family put away their mourning garb, but Mehrangiz continued to wear her black scarf. Ali's mother had not succeeded in throwing her out, but she persisted in her threats and in her confrontations with Ali. In early fall, the marriage of the younger sister to the same suitor Father had rejected was solemnized. Monavvar Khanom and Nayyer stayed seven days and nights in the bride's house.

In the afternoons the youngsters would gather in the old nursery with Mehrangiz. The older sister seemed thoughtful and kept her lips sealed. The younger sister, her cheeks rosy, her face hairs removed and her eyebrows plucked into an arch, had become someone altogether different. The smile never left her lips. Although Nayyer now covered her face from Ali, every time she twisted and rolled with laughter the *chador* slipped from her head. She was grown and had become coy.

Ali would begin to imitate someone or other. The older sister never smiled, even when everyone else was doubled over with laughter. Ali imitated everyone except her.

One day Ali was holding a long stick in his hand, pointing to the wall that was his imaginary geographical map. First he imitated the history teacher, then the geography teacher, and then he mixed the two lessons. He was saying, "This long and narrow strip is Egypt, and here is the River Nile. The Egyptian pharaohs considered themselves gods. They made mountains like God's mountains, so they could climb up from them to the sky."

The older sister frowned and interrupted Ali: "Ali, that's blasphemy. Ask God's pardon!"

Nayyer said, "Ezzat, dear, we're just playing. It's entertaining. Is that wrong?"

"Playing? Are you children? If Ali were married, his son would be my age."

Mehrangiz said, "God willing, Ali Aqa will marry. I'll raise his child myself. And as for you, Ezzat Khanom, you'll go to a husband's house, not this year but the next. I have a premonition."

Ezzat Khanom said nothing more. Nayyer said, "Ali Aqa, you were saying they built mountains . . . "

Ali continued, "Yes, but building mountains is no easy job. And human beings are not God to build mountains in the twinkling of an eye—to say, 'Be!' and have it so. These mountains were built by the slaves. Many of them died under the hot sun and the stroke of the whip. And many others piled the rocks one atop the other and—heave ho!—kept going higher. Now, not only could the pharaohs not reach the sky, they died right here on earth. Then they mummified them and buried them in the heart of these mountains."

Mehrangiz, eyes wide with wonder, asked, "Aqa, are the people of Egypt black?"

Ali said, "No, Mehrangiz, they're not black, but it's not only blacks who are treated cruelly."

Ali's mother sold the mantelpiece clock in the parlor with the statuettes of black girls on either side. The money went into the trousseau and was sent with the younger sister to her husband's house. Although the younger sister was married off, and despite the fact that the master of the accounting house had made Ali his secretary, the family was living from hand to mouth. Mother's threats about Mehrangiz being an extra mouth to feed continued. Whenever Mehrangiz found a chance, she picked Ali's brains for details about the dead Egyptians. "How come they haven't turned into dust? How, Aqa? Did they bring the blacks from Egypt? Does Egypt have a river? Sweetheart, you said yourself there was a river everywhere. I heard Nur ol-Saba's city was below Egypt, a city just like paradise. Nur ol-Saba was the princess of this same city."

Ali's mother sold the large copper pot in which, on the anniversary of the martyrdom of Imam Hasan, they cooked saffron pudding as an oblation. She gave half the money to an old crone who had made the match; the other half went into the first-day party for the newly married sister. The day of the party, Ali did not go to work but entertained the guests. Nayyer and Monavvar Khanom were busy laying out slivers of fried eggplants around the rice and flattering the bridegroom's family. Mother had her hands on her hips and, as usual, was giving Mehrangiz minute instructions. Mehrangiz was spinning like a top—fetching things, taking them away, serving the guests. The guests left before dark, but Monavvar Khanom and Nayyer stayed. Ali lay on the carpet in the large room. Nayyer was praying in the same room. Her cheeks were rosy and her glance was fixed on Ali. They looked each other directly in the eye. Mehrangiz had slipped into the room so quietly Ali had not noticed. He felt her hand on his arm. She whispered in his ear, "Aqa, come with me." Ali was tired and loath to leave Nayyer with her round face and shy, laughing eyes. But this woman had raised him. She was closer to him than his mother. He followed her. They stood behind the closed door of the parlor and listened. Monavvar Khanom's voice was heard clearly: "He's a good suitor, but the promise . . . "

Ali didn't hear the rest of what she said. The gurgling of the hookah interfered. It was his mother smoking. Mother answered, "Let's see what fate ordains."

Monavvar Khanom said something, but only a couple of words were audible: "Hand in hand . . . " Mother's answer shed light on the meaning of her words: "Sister, I absolutely don't expect you to wait for us. You know we can't even make ends meet on Ali's salary, much less take in a daughter-in-law as well."

"I thought they might be in love. Isn't it a pity?"

Mother answered harshly, "Ali is still a child. He's got a long way to go before he's in love."

Monavvar Khanom's answer was clear: "I told you so that you wouldn't complain later."

Ali dressed hurriedly and, without bidding Monavvar Khanom and Nayyer good-bye, left them. As Mehrangiz held the door, she said, "Don't you grieve, Aqa, all right? Grief dries up a man's roots."

Ali stood at the door and said, "Should I go into the room right now and tell them Nayyer is mine? They have no right to marry her off. Should I tell them Nayyer has been with me since childhood? Nayyer has always been with me."

He turned, but Mehrangiz stopped him and said, "Aqa, Madam will get upset. She'll start a fight. Things will go from bad to worse . . . " She continued, "If I had a black crêpe de Chine *chador*, I'd put it on and go to Monavvar Khanom's house and say, 'Monavvar Khanom, my Aqa . . . ' What would be the right thing to say, sweetheart?"

One afternoon Ali knocked on the door but no one opened it. He could hear curses and weeping from within. Agitated, Ali knocked harder. His sister finally opened the door. Ali walked in. He saw Mehrangiz spread out on the ground in the yard, her forehead split open and the big kitchen knife glittering by the edge of the pool. Ali looked at his mother, who was trembling and apparently terror-stricken. A lump formed in Ali's throat and he asked, "What's going on? For God's sake, what's going on?"

Mother said, "There's no room here for me and this Mombasa nigger servant. All of you prefer this ugly creature to me. Like father, like son. I know you'll find your way to her, too."

Dumbstruck, Ali stared at his mother. "For God's sake, cut it out. What happened?"

"Nothing. What did you expect? Look here." And she put two pieces of wax stuck together in Ali's hand. Ali didn't quite understand what these two pieces of wax were. He gazed in wonder first at Mother, then at his sister, and finally at Mehrangiz, who was still lying on the ground and moaning. Mother said, "Yes, now she's up to witchcraft. I found these two dolls stuck together in the kitchen. I ask her, 'What are these?' She says, 'They're for Aqa and Nayyer Khanom so they'll come together.' What do you take me for? You think I don't know you, you old hag? If you know witchcraft, why don't you do it for this girl so her fortune will turn? Huh? Then I tell her, 'You've got to get out of this house right now before Ali gets back.' She picks up the knife to kill me."

Mehrangiz was now sitting, bleeding and muddy. She said, "Aqa, I couldn't take what Madam was saying. I picked up the knife to kill myself, to put myself out of my misery. I, worthless nigger that I am, who am I to kill Madam or have wicked designs on my child? I've turned old in this household . . . " Tears prevented her from continuing.

When Ali came home that night, he saw Mehrangiz sitting on the bench outside their door with a bundle at her side. Seeing Ali, she burst into tears, "I've got to go now. Madam says such terrible things. Anyone who attributes such things to her own child has the right to say anything she wants to me, a nigger servant. Sweetheart, take these two wax dolls, tie something heavy to them, then drop them in the pool. By next week, Nayyer will be yours. I've got to say good-bye now. Sweetheart, I raised you. I—"

"Where are you going now? Where do you have to go?"

Mehrangiz wiped her tears and said, "Don't worry about me, Aqa. I'll go to Monavvar Khanom's house. God willing, I'll become the prize of Nayyer Khanom's trousseau. We'll come back to your house together; we'll be with my own Aqa. Sweetheart, I'm the dust under your feet. But if Monavvar Khanom doesn't take me in, sweetheart, I'll sit near the cobblers' bazaar and beg. Come visit me sometime, will you?"

Nayyer was married a few months later. Mehrangiz became the prize of her trousseau and went with her to the bridegroom's house. But the bridegroom wasn't Ali. Monavvar Khanom and Nayyer came to Ali's house to offer the invitations and bid farewell. He didn't show himself and, despite his mother's insistence, didn't attend the wedding. Nayyer's wedding night was the first night in a while that Ali could not sleep. He thought something had fallen on his mattress. He got up several times to check it, but there was nothing there.

The next day before noon there was a knock on the door. Ali wasn't expecting his mother and sister; they wouldn't have left the wedding so early. He opened the door to find Mehrangiz, wearing a black crêpe de Chine *chador*, though it was old. They went to the large room together. Mehrangiz brought out a bundled handkerchief from under her *chador* and put it in front of Ali ceremoniously. It held a plate of sweets wrapped in a floral silk head scarf.

Ali asked, "What's this?"

"Aqa, I was thinking of you again. These are wedding sweets."

Ali was depressed. To break the silence, he asked, "You left the bride and bridegroom to come here?"

"I asked Nayyer Khanom's permission."

Ali remained silent. Mehrangiz said, "The bridegroom is bald. I didn't see it last night, you know. Last night in the bridal chamber he had a hat on. In the morning when I went to make their bed I saw him. He's perfectly bald. He's a police officer. Seems to me he could be a wrestler too. My own Aqa's pinky is worth a hundred such bridegrooms."

A lump had formed in Ali's throat. He asked, "How's Nayyer? Was she happy?"

Mehrangiz shook her head. Her lip hung low, as though she were going to cry. She said, "No. Last night in the bridal chamber she was sitting on the bed. However much the ladies said, 'Come, give your hand . . . ' You see, they wanted to make them hold hands. But she wouldn't give her hand. The ladies were saying, 'She wants a veil.' No, Aqa. Nayyer Khanom didn't want a veil. But she was so pretty, you know. They'd put geraniums in her hair and among the flowers was a light bulb. Don't ask me how. Good Lord! Any time Nayyer Khanom wanted to turn out the light bulb, she could. The battery was in her own hand. Sweetheart, finally the bridegroom used brute force and took Nayyer Khanom's hand. One of the geraniums fell on the bed."

~~~~~~

Nayyer and her son Bijan would sometimes come to Ali's house with Mehrangiz. But in the few years since the police officer had joined the family, he had never come visiting, except at new year. He had not exchanged two words with Ali. Nayyer had made her son an army uniform. Although the child seemed uncomfortable in the military outfit, he'd puff out his chest. When he walked, his little wooden sword struck his leg. Ali had asked Nayyer once, "Are you already teaching him these things?" Nayyer had said, "Cute, isn't he?" And Ali had relented. But Nayyer never again dressed Bijan in the army uniform when they came to Ali's house.

The captain was away on a mission and Nayyer and Mehrangiz and Bijan stayed to lunch at Ali's house. Nayyer had gained weight and her face was uncovered. Every time she laughed, her cheeks dimpled. But when her glance fell on Ali, it was sad and plaintive. Every afternoon Ezzat Khanom stood to pray in the parlor. She had become very pious and said long prayers.

After lunch Mehrangiz brought Bijan to the large room to put him to sleep. Ali was lying down there, reading the paper. Mehrangiz was so old now that even Ali's mother had stopped believing that Ali would find a way to her.

Ali laid aside the paper and became engrossed in Bijan's mannerisms, so reminiscent of Nayyer's as a child. Bijan was being mischievous, refusing to sleep. He wanted a picture book, which Ali did not have. Or at least a color pencil and a piece of paper. Mehrangiz said, "Bijan Khan, go kiss Aqa and then I'll tell you a story so you'll sleep. If you don't sleep in this heat, you'll get heatstroke again, you know." Ali closed his eyes in anticipation of Bijan's kiss, but the kiss didn't come.

Ali heard Mehrangiz's hushed voice: "They bowed to Nur ol-Saba. They bowed to her over and over again. They dressed her in satin gowns and put jewels on her. Then they took her to their own city. In their own city, sweetheart, there was a king who made the blacks build mountains for him by the river. Their city had everything except a mountain. Their king wanted a mountain, you see. The blacks put five-hundred-pound rocks on their backs and took them to build the mountain. Now Nur ol-Saba sees those mountains. But no trees grow on those mountains, you know . . . "

Ali opened his eyes. He saw Mehrangiz sitting by Bijan, her hand under his shirt, rubbing his back. He asked, "Mehrangiz, why don't trees grow?"

78

Mehrangiz said, "Aqa, I disturbed your sleep. Bijan Khan doesn't sleep unless I tell him stories, just like you."

"I asked, why don't trees grow?"

"So much blood was shed at the foot of these mountains. Aqa, the blood of black cats and black men brings bad luck."

Ali shut his eyes. He heard Bijan say, "More, more." And again it was the voice of Mehrangiz and the old familiar stories of the riverside and the man in the kaffiyeh and headband. Then came a story Ali had never heard.

"My mammy knew the language of the blacks, but nobody taught me. One day a black man comes to Aqa Ali's grandfather's house and talks to my mammy in their own language. Madam and Aqa had no idea what he was saying. Next day my mammy puts her bundle under her arm. She says, 'I'm going to the bath.' She goes. No one hears from her for a year. They search everywhere. You'd think she'd melted and sunk into the earth. Everybody was saying, 'The nigger's escaped.' One day at dusk she comes back. But she's not alone. I'm with her. She's swaddled me in cloth and hidden me under her *chador*. She cries and cries, and Madam forgives her. Then every year she takes me away and disappears for a few days . . . "

Ali sat up and asked, "Mehrangiz, do you remember where she went? Who'd she go to?"

Mehrangiz said, "I remember a few things, like in a dream. We used to go to a well. A man would come and hold me in his arms. He'd kiss me. He'd pick fresh cucumbers and give them to me. Then I'd stay with the cows. I was afraid of the cows, turning, turning all the time. But I remember when the bucket came up the well full of water and the water spilled down with a sound, I was happy. The wheel was singing all the time and the water was falling with a sound. My mammy and the man would go into a room and shut the door on themselves. The last year that we went, the man wasn't there. There was a man who told my mammy, 'They've found him. They've put him in chains and taken him to Bushehr. My mammy cried . . . "

One evening as the sun went down Ali put on his clothes and was about to leave the house when there was an urgent knocking at the door. It was Nayyer's husband with the stars on his shoulders and epaulettes and chevrons and truncheon. So the captain had returned from his mission. Ali's heart sank. Sometimes he felt such an aversion to the man that he wanted to pluck the stars off his shoulders, and the epaulettes and the chevrons, toss them away, grab the truncheon out of his hand and club him on the head with it. At other times, he felt a strange affection for him. After all, he was closer to Nayyer than anyone else. Ali stood waiting, afraid to start the conversation. Nayyer's husband said, "Come with me. Just you alone." Ali's apprehension intensified. To himself he thought, "Which is it, Nayyer or Mehrangiz?" He wanted to snatch the truncheon out of the captain's hand. He asked at last, "What's the matter?"

They walked together. Ali had never gone to Nayyer's house. His heart was pounding.

He asked again, "What's the matter? Why do you want me to come alone?"

"My orderly didn't know your place. I had to come myself."

Ali asked, "Is my cousin all right? How's Mehrangiz? Your son Bijan . . . " The police officer said, "Mehrangiz has asked to see you. The old woman has gotten daft. She overpumped the Primus stove and the stove exploded. She's burned from head to foot. It's been a few days now."

"Where is she now? In the hospital?"

The police officer said, "It wasn't worth the trouble."

Ali fell silent and said no more until they reached Nayyer's house. Nayyer opened the door. Her belly was swollen again and she held Bijan by the hand. Her eyes were red. She said to Ali, "She's in the attic. I was too scared to remain at her side alone."

Ali went up the steps. The door was open. Inside, Mehrangiz was collapsed in a heap on a mattress. Her face was so swollen that she could hardly open her eyes. When she saw Ali, a faint smile broke upon her lips and she said, "I was waiting for you, my Aqa."

"Why didn't you send me word sooner?" Ali said. "I'd have brought you a doctor. I'd have taken you to the hospital."

"What's the use, Aqa?"

Ali saw that Mehrangiz was trying to pull herself toward the southern window of the room. He asked, "Should I open the window?"

"No, Aqa, I want to face Mecca . . . "

When she lay still again, Ali dragged the mattress to face the window.

Nayyer came in, a white handkerchief in her hand. Mehrangiz seemed calm. She said to Nayyer, "Madam, the prayer tablet is on the shelf. Take it and put it on my eyes."

Nayyer took the prayer tablet from the shelf. She blew the dust away and said, "This prayer tablet's broken. Let me get you a whole one."

"Let it be. Let it be broken. They say the nigger was blind in one eye, so they put a broken prayer tablet on her eyes."

Ali sat on the floor by Mehrangiz's mattress. Nayyer said: "Should I go get you a chair?"

"No, no."

Then silence. Nayyer remained standing, weeping quietly. She moved her hand and turned the light switch. A dusty light bulb came on. Then they heard Mehrangiz's voice, softly, as if it were coming from another world: "They dyed my feet with henna. I felt cool. I got into the carriage with Nur ol-Saba. The men had fur hats. It was the Fath al-Eyaleh well. He picked fresh cucumbers for me. So cool, cool, cool. How cool in your belly . . . He cleaned and arranged my bed. Said she was going to the bath. She's gone to the bath . . . my child will tie my chin . . . I was scared to tie her chin—her mouth had gotten twisted, completely crooked, crooked. The blacks built the mountains. Under the mountains there's a city like paradise. We'll go there, you know. Cool, cool, cool water . . . "

Ali was sitting by Mehrangiz's corpse. Nayyer was standing, her belly prominent. The shadow she cast on the wall resembled a pyramid resting on its side.

# انیس

# Anis

Batul Khanom herself answered the knock at the door and was startled at the sight of Anis, who wore two mounds of rouge on her cheeks, black rubber boots, and a clinging red dress that generously displayed her knees and part of her thighs. No prayer *chador* or the white head scarf that she'd always worn, the two ends wrapped and crossed over her shoulders—with which, and without any makeup, she resembled the Virgin Mary. It was unheard of for Anis to go without long, black twill pants under her dress. And what a pity for all that luxuriant hair, which she now wore in a boyish cut! Batul Khanom opened her mouth to ask, "Anis, why have you done this to yourself?" when a tall, fat man in jeans and a floral shirt with the upper buttons undone appeared. He walked in and

85

said, "Hi. Pleased to meet you." Reaching for Batul Khanom's hand, he pressed it firmly. Bending down, he untied his shoe-laces and took off his shoes.

They sat on chairs at the dining table. Batul Khanom saw that Anis was not wearing her gold bangles. She hardly knew what to say or where to begin.

Mohammad Aqa said, "Anis Soltan has sung your praises a lot."

On his wrist he wore a watch with a dark dial and an array of red markings, and from his neck hung a gold chain. The hair on his chest showed, and the "Allah" pendant at the mid-point of the chain rested squarely where his shirt was buttoned. Anis went out to brew tea, and Batul Khanom thought, What a fool I was to help her get divorced! I got not only myself into a bind, but her as well. I suppose I'll have to arrange her divorce myself this time, too.

She asked him, "So, Mohammad Aqa, what do you do for a living?"

He answered, "My trade is lawful."

"Anis has worked for me for six years. She's seen a lot of hardship. I want to ensure her happiness."

"I can feed my wife and children," he said. "If I couldn't, do you think I'd have stepped up?"

He spoke in a staccato, fixing his eyes on Batul Khanom's. Anis brought in the tea and said, "Madam, Mohammad Aqa can do all sorts of jobs." She paused, then continued, "I wish you could have been there last night. He took me to the New Blossom nightclub . . . ooh, what a dancer that Nadia is!"

Batul Khanom said to Mohammad Aqa, "My son and daughter are in America. I look upon Anis as my own child."

Anis laughed and said, "Mohammad Aqa, I told you Madam is a high school teacher, didn't I? When she'd come home from school every day, she'd ask, 'Anis, any letters from the kids?' But unless I got a payoff . . . "

Batul Khanom said, "Have you told Mohammad Aqa you're a widow and a divorcee and your period of separation hasn't ended yet? Have you told him you're twenty-six years old?"

Mohammad Aqa, apparently, was not moved by this in the least, but Anis frowned and said, "Now did you have to go and mention that?"

Batul Khanom said, "I beg your pardon, it certainly merits mentioning. Why don't you sit down now and tell him everything, from A to Z?" To herself she thought, If this marriage falls through, it'll be better for both of us—I am awfully tired.

Anis maintained an indignant silence. Batul Khanom said, "My dear girl, I'm only looking out for you."

Mohammad Aqa said, "I swear on my own head, Anis Khanom, when Mr. Kazeminizadeh was describing you to me, I fell in love with you. I'm not going to give you up. It's all the same to me."

Anis lowered her head. "In the village of Ayenevarzan, my father was a peddler. I was married to Mashhadi Baqer, the butcher. In our village, even before fall came around, tempers would flare and the fights would begin. Clubs, crowbars, spades—they'd go at each other, you know. One of the ringleaders was my brother, and the other ringleader was my brother-in-law."

Mohammad Aqa pulled out a mother-of-pearl cigarette box, opened it, and held it in front of Batul Khanom. Batul Khanom wanted a cigarette. Whenever the children's letters were late in coming she'd smoke two packs of Zars a day. But now she held back. She wanted to take nothing from a man who, her heart declared, had led Anis astray and who would make Anis miserable even if he did marry her. The rooms had not been swept in a week. If only Mohammad Aqa would get the hell out.

He put a cigarette to his lips and pulled out a lighter from the pocket of his jeans. The lighter looked like a woman's, flecked with glittering stones. Anis took the ashtray from the middle of the table and put it in front of Mohammad Aqa. He gave his lighted cigarette to Anis and said, "Take a puff." Anis puffed and coughed, puffed and coughed. Batul Khanom thought, She's putting on an act. She said, "You were saying, Anis?"

Anis snuffed out the cigarette in the ashtray and said, "What can I say, when silence is better? You know, 'Know your own pain rather than another's.'"

Batul Khanom was looking at Anis intently. Her prominent cheeks had turned deep red, either from rouge or a blush, and her round chin was trembling. Her dark, fawn-like eyes were wet. Batul Khanom thought, It's no wonder she's got the fellow running after her . . . her mouth is a bit wide, and her teeth protrude a little, like a rabbit's, and she's dark, but what of it? She has a mole near her lip that's worth all the gold in China.

Batul Khanom would not let up. Anis had to lay out her own pain rather than another's once again. But Batul Khanom and her husband knew it all, and so did all the folks in Ayenevarzan. What did it mean other than that she was putting on airs?

"When the fight began, my brother wasn't in the village, you know. He'd gone to Damavand. It was sundown when he got back home. I said, 'Brother, the fight's begun. Aren't you going?' My brother said, 'Empty handed?' There was a crowbar in the yard. I put it in his hand. Turns out my brother accidentally knocks my brother-in-law in the head with the crowbar."

Mohammad Aqa sat upright and asked, "Your brother killed your ex-brother-in-law? Where's he now? In jail?"

Batul Khanom was grateful that the fellow was scared. She wanted him to change his mind so Anis would stay with her for a while longer, until she had a chance to find another suitable maid. No one had watered the flowers in the flower beds for three days now.

Anis said, "No, he didn't die, you know. They took him to the hospital. Now he's crazy . . . and then Mashhadi Baqer came home very late. His eyes looked daggers. He kicked me in the ribs, then slaps and punches and smacks me on the head. He spat in my face and said, 'Get out. Go until your hair turns as white as your teeth. I won't give you a divorce.'"

Anis started to cry. "Sakineh and my mother and I left in the dead of night—through mountains and valleys and crags."

Mohammad Aqa said, "What's past is past. I'll see you never have to worry about a thing. I'll talk to you soft as a rose."

Anis raised her head coquettishly and asked with a wink, "When we quarrel, what'll you beat me with, then?"

Mohammad Aqa bit his lip.

Anis said, "Batul Khanom, you're no stranger. Mohammad Aqa calls me Khaleh Suskeh. He says, 'I'll beat you with my soft and satiny tail.'" She giggled. Then she put her mouth to Batul Khanom's ear and said, "Mohammad Aqa says, 'If these are breasts, how come they fill the dress?'"

Batul Khanom glared at Anis. "Girl, have some shame!" she scolded.

Maybe, Batul Khanom thought, what she had sensed was not true. Maybe Mohammad Aqa would turn out to be a good man. You can't judge a man in a single encounter. I hope I'm not jealous that Anis has landed herself an attractive man and they want each other. Anis is changed completely. Her eyes, her lips are laughing . . . but this Mohammad Aqa that I see is one of those slippery ones. Very likely he's made Anis sell her gold bangles. Let's hope to God he hasn't gone after her savings. Anis has close to twenty-eight thousand *tuman*s . . .

Anis's voice interrupted her thoughts: "My dear Mohammad Aqa, you don't know what sufferings I've endured! I'm sure God has sent you my way in return for all my miseries— if there *is* a God, as Miss Goli says. We got on the bus in Damavand and came to Tehran. Near the depot on Naser Khosrow Avenue there was an old man sitting in a chair smoking. He set up my mother and Sakineh in a couple's house with six kids. Now Sakineh's married—what a fine husband! Of course, not better than you. Mr. Kazeminizadeh found him. He came at once and took our first month's wages."

Batul Khanom asked, "Anis, what does your brother-in-law do?"

"Runs odd jobs in a real estate agency right by New Lalezar."

In those days, Anis admitted, she'd been comfortable in Batul Khanom's household. Miss Goli hadn't gone to America yet. Late afternoons she'd go with Miss Goli for a stroll in

Ferdowsi Square. She'd shop on Shahreza Avenue. Until the Family Protection Law was passed.

Anis shook her head and said, "Ah, life! After six years I saw Mashhadi Baqer again just three months ago. He was yelling in the courtroom, 'She's been rebellious! Everyone knows that her brother has wrecked my brother's life!' But Madam here wasn't yelling. She said, 'Your honor, he hasn't paid any wife support for six years.' If it hadn't been for Aqa's say-so, things wouldn't have happened so quickly. Then when we came out of the courtroom and Madam had put my divorce papers in her bag, I turned to Mashhadi Baqer and said, 'See, Mashhadi Baqer, see how your hair turned white, but mine's still black?' Outside he said, 'I'll deal with you yet.'"

Although Anis believed that Mashhadi Baqer was more bark than bite and had no gumption for revenge, after the divorce she thought and talked of nothing but a husband. She was looking left and right for a husband, until finally she went pleading to Mr. Kazeminizadeh.

Turning to Mohammad Aqa, Batul Khanom asked, "Well, what about the bride money? How much are you offering?"

Anis brought in fruit and put it on the table. She asked Mohammad Aqa, "Shall I peel a pomegranate for you? Poor darling! You need something cool. Last night . . . "

"I'll have a cucumber," he said. He took a knife with a mother-of-pearl handle from his pocket and busied himself with peeling the cucumber.

Batul Khanom said, "I asked, how much bride money are you offering?"

He sprinkled salt on his cucumber and said, "Anis Soltan hasn't asked for bride money. She's asked for a Koran, a loaf of rock sugar, and a book . . . I can't remember the name now."

Batul Khanom asked, "Anis, what's this about a book? You can't read."

Anis said, "That same book that Parichehr Khanom got when she was married."

Batul Khanom lost her temper. "What impudence from someone like you! That book was Ferdowsi's *Book of Kings*." Turning to Mohammad Aqa she said, "You must offer no less than five thousand *tuman*s."

Mohammad Aqa said, "I don't like for people to order my wife around and curse and swear. She's left your service; she's not your maid. Besides, who's to offer bride money, and who's to accept?"

Anis said, "Madam dear, Mohammad Aqa is owed some money. When he gets it he'll buy me everything. We've seen a gold necklace . . . "

Batul Khanom said quietly, "Even a mother and daughter sometimes fight. Anis doesn't take offense at what I say." She turned to Anis and asked, "What did you do with your gold bangles?"

She noticed Mohammad Aqa motioning to Anis with his eyebrows. Anis said, "I pawned my bangles." Batul Khanom finished the rest: "And I bought all this junk. I went to the New Blossom nightclub, I bought Mohammad Aqa a gold chain and a woman's lighter—what else? Did you think I was born yesterday?"

"For now I've started Mohammad Aqa in his business. One of these days the money he's owed—"

"Heaven help us all!" Mohammad Aqa said. "Now look what I've gotten myself into."

Batul Khanom said, "Better an early war than a late peace."

Mohammad Aqa said, "The only gift Anis Soltan has bought me are these brass knuckles," whereupon he took the knuckles out of his back pocket and put them on the table. "Here they are," he said.

Batul Khanom's husband arrived, and though his eyes were glazed over with fatigue, he affably exchanged small talk with Mohammad Aqa. Finally, he cautioned Anis against hurrying and convinced them both that, since Madam was all alone, Anis should stay with them until the end of her period of separation.

As Mohammad Aqa turned to go he said, "Excuse me, but the woman's willing, the man's willing . . . " Leaving his sentence unfinished, he said, "So long."

With Mohammad Aqa gone, Batul Khanom shouted, "Where in blazing hell do you pick up these bizarre characters? He's come courting with brass knuckles!"

Anis said, "Oh, the funny things he does!" She hesitated, then continued, "In my mother's boss's house he called his partner about the money he's owed. I put my hand on his shoulder—he turned his head and kissed my hand twice."

Batul Khanom said, "You've served me for six years. You were wallowing in the gutter when you first got here. I won't see you miserable again. This man has his eyes on your money. He's not the marrying kind."

Anis said, "Didn't Miss Goli used to say, 'I'll only marry the man I love'?" After a pause she said, "I swear to God, Madam, you're jealous."

Batul Khanom let out a yell: "Shut up, you hussy!"

Aqa called from his study, "Keep it down, will you?"

Batul Khanom calmed herself and said, "Last time I got your divorce myself, but this time there'll be none of that."

Anis said, "Who can blame that wretch? All his hair had turned white. Anyway, he was my first lucky draw."

"Do you want me to mediate so you and that same Mash-hadi Baqer can be reconciled?"

"God forbid! Do you think I'm out of my mind?"

The first year Anis had come to work for Batul Khanom, she'd chosen any and every occasion to relate her life story and weep and blame herself. She'd said if she hadn't given her brother the crowbar that day at sundown, if she hadn't sent him to the fight but adjured him to stay home, she wouldn't have lost everything, and her brother-in-law wouldn't have gone crazy. How many people had paid the price for her naiveté!

Once Anis took to city life, husband and sense of guilt and naiveté and remorse were all forgotten, to be replaced by radio, television, Mr. Fardin's films, and getting chummy with the shopkeepers. How was it possible now for her to return to the village and stay there and become of one soul and one purpose with Mashhadi Baqer, who always smelled of raw meat—Anis, who for six years had sat in front of the television every night, by whose ear the radio had played constantly, who had shopped on Shahreza Avenue, who had bought the choicest cuts of meat from the butcher and the crispest loaves of bread from the baker, who had flirted with Salar's gardener, who had gone to Ramsar Cinema with Miss Goli, who had seen *Joseph and Zolaykha* and fallen in love with the Turkish actor Fakhreddin, Fakhreddin later being supplanted by Mr. Fardin, each of whose films she had seen twice, three times. Now how could she be reconciled with Mashhadi Baqer and go back to the village and adjust herself to cow dung and kerosene lamps and no television, especially now that God had sent her Mohammad Aqa, who had kissed her hand twice and who had neither bad breath nor smelly feet?

Anis kept a vigil for long hours outside Mr. Fardin's door so she could catch a glimpse of her favorite star. Once, she had gone in, only to learn that he was away in Abadan. She had come home and, without Batul Khanom's permission, had cooked a farewell broth and given it to the neighbors. Mr. Fardin's pictures were on the walls of her room, under her pillow, everywhere. It's true, Anis was never slack about praying and fasting, but after her prayers she prayed to Mr. Fardin. Now she was in love with Mohammad Aqa, who looked like Vahdat, the Isfahani actor, minus that personality of his that came through in the movies. Besides, he was taller than Vahdat.

"Really, Madam, thank you indeed! Give up Mohammad Aqa and go back to the village?"

Every day at noon when Batul Khanom returned from school she spun and wove. And in the afternoon, Mohammad Aqa would telephone and Batul Khanom would watch her work come unraveled. First Anis would turn pale, then flush red and laugh hysterically, then call him sweet things: "I swear, I feel exactly the same . . . no, no, not at all . . . it's nothing, really . . . anything you say."

Several times Batul Khanom was tempted to snatch the telephone from Anis and send a few curses Mohammad Aqa's way, but she thought it beneath her dignity to bandy words with him. After Mohammad Aqa's call, Anis would go limp.

Anis swore that God had never created a wittier creature than Mohammad Aqa. He imitated all the singers, wore his hat at a tilt, and sang street songs and spoke in dialect—Isfahani, Turkish, Rashti, Gilaki. You could split your sides with laughter listening to him. Once he had raced Anis around the garden of her mother's boss's house. Taking his clothes off, he had won the race in his underwear with only his shoes and socks on. Her mother and Sakineh had clutched their bellies and laughed and laughed. So what if he couldn't redeem Anis's bangles from hock? To hell with them! So what if, as Batul Khanom anticipated, he spent the twenty-eight thousand *tuman*s she had saved up? To hell with the money! What did it matter if they had to scrape the bottom of the barrel and spend all of Anis's worldly possessions on nightclubs and vodka and movies and kabob and liver and head and trotters soup at Tajrish Bridge? Who better for it all to go to? It was worth it. After all, you only live once.

Batul Khanom would say, "I don't know, really." Then it would suddenly sink in, "Oh, so he guzzles booze, too, damn him, and no doubt has you join in?"

Anis lasted in Batul Khanom's house no more than two weeks, and even then she couldn't put her mind and heart into the work. She had become sloppy. Once the cats stole a pound of boneless meat from the kitchen table and she didn't notice. They took the meat to the rooftop, and their fighting and caterwauling didn't let Batul Khanom and her husband sleep a wink until the morning call to prayer—once your sleep is broken, how are you going to doze off again? She was careless in her dusting—one spot on the sofa shone like a bald pate and another was covered in dust. Every day the food was either too salty or tasteless. She'd say she couldn't bear to be away from Mohammad Aqa anymore. If he didn't call one day, she'd bawl and cry her eyes out: "I swear to God, Madam, I can't help it." No, she didn't know what he did or who his mother and sister were. But there were no two ways about it, she'd either do away with herself or with Mohammad Aqa. The good thing about Mohammad Aqa was that he could cheer her up. It was as though she were in a pleasant dream; at the sound of his footsteps, her heart skipped a beat. He'd say, "You're free. Don't wear the head scarf; don't let it get you down. Wear a short-sleeved blouse so your arms feel the air."

When it came time to go, she asked Batul Khanom, "Madam, would you hold my wedding here?"

Batul Khanom said, "Not with Mohammad Aqa."

≫ ≫ ≫

To Anis it was well worth it. It was worth it to be in bliss for forty days and savor all the world's delights, and then for "the camel to die and Haji to go free." Mohammad Aqa did not die, of course; they parted on friendly terms. All that was left to Anis were her gold teeth. That was all.

As for Hosayn Aqa, dear man, Batul Khanom found him and had them married in her own house. Hosayn Aqa wore a loose-fitting grey robe that reached his ankles. He wore a white skullcap and was constantly fingering his worry beads. He was Imam Hosayn's eulogist. The first thing he did was to buy Anis a black *chador*, a full-length dress and two pairs of thick black stockings. That was it. He could afford no more.

Hosayn Aqa would give Anis directions and she would rush to the graveside or funeral service. As soon as Hosayn Aqa raised his voice, Anis would start wailing so pathetically that the most hard-hearted of the listeners would burst into tears, and the women would ask among themselves, "What is this lady's relationship to the deceased?"

They lived in a garage in Batul Khanom's neighborhood, serving as caretakers for the owner of the house, who had emigrated to America with his family, and who returned once a year to collect his pension, debts, and the interest from his savings deposit and to leave the utility money with Batul Khanom. Anis held the keys to the rooms and swept and dusted once a week. Both Hosayn Aqa and the house-sitting were fixed up by Batul Khanom, whom Anis visited frequently, cleaning her vegetables and washing and ironing her clothes. The money helped. Hosayn Aqa thought it wrong to start up the landlord's refrigerator, stove, and washing machine.

Now Anis had taken to covering her face from anybody and everybody—from the fish in the pond and the pigeons on the roof and Batul Khanom's husband. When she talked with the shopkeepers she altered her voice. The cats frequented her house for a time, but since there was nothing to be had there they gave thanks for Batul Khanom's kitchen. Even in the middle of summer Anis had her thick black stockings on.

Instead of a white head scarf, she wore a black veil, which she had made herself, that showed only the oval of her face. If they couldn't land any burials, funerals, or memorial ceremonies for the seventh and fortieth nights, they were in bad shape. Anis would go to Batul Khanom's house with a bowl and knock on her door to ask for ice. Batul Khanom, who now had a new maid, would sense that the going was tough and give Anis the leftovers from yesterday's lunch or last night's dinner to take home. Anis would pick little red radishes and basil and marjoram from Batul Khanom's garden and lay out such a spread for dear Hosayn Aqa that she would start admiring it herself. As soon as Hosayn Aqa came home, she'd say, "I missed you." She'd clean the dust from his shoes and say, "Don't you worry, all right? God himself is the provider."

Batul Khanom wrote a note to Mr. Mo'ini, the custodian of her mother's grave in the shrine of Abol-Azim, commending Hosayn Aqa to him. Mr. Mo'ini allowed Hosayn Aqa to recite the commemorative prayer at the entrance to the shrine every Friday night, to occasionally sing the mourning song, *rawza*, and, when no corpses came his way, to sell prayer tablets, beads, candles, icons, and pictures of Mecca in Bagh-e Tuti or by the bazaar. Anis hit a lucky streak and their business picked up. Every Tuesday they held a women's *rawza* in the garage where they lived. Little by little, in response to demands from supplicants and oblationers, they began laying out ceremonial food offering *sofra*s, too. Batul Khanom gave her approval for opening up the reception room of the house and holding the *rawza* and the *sofra* there. She even said the landlord, too, would reap blessings and win God's favor.

As for the Roqiyeh *sofra*, it was the saddest of all. The poor made special requests, pleading with Roqiyeh to ease their pains and cure their children. Anis would spread a small *sofra* in the corner of the garage with bread, cheese, greens, and dates neatly arranged. Then she'd light a candle and stand it up on a tin can cover. The petitioner, her relatives, and Batul Khanom would come and sit around the *sofra*. The child, either cured or still unwell, would sit in his mother's arms as Anis recited Roqiyeh's *rawza* and everyone wept heartily. The child, too, would start to cry and fuss until they put a date in his mouth, after which he'd calm down. Anis would say to the petitioner, "May God accept your oblation." The other women would say to Anis, "Please say prayers for us," and Anis would reply, "I'm in need of yours."

But Anis set up the Abol-Fazl and Imam Hasan *sofra*s and the Imam's birthday with complete rites in the landlord's reception room. She'd taken all the portraits off the walls, wrapped them in a large bedsheet, and put them on the dining table. Then she'd laid out candles, roses, halva for pregnant women, noodle soup, lentil rice, fruits, good-luck nuts . . . She knew everything on Imam Hosayn's *sofra* had to be green, and that she herself had to be dressed in green and wear a green silk prayer *chador*, but there were few takers for Imam

Hosayn's *sofra*, and Hosayn Aqa thought it sinful to spend wastefully. So Anis had bought a green silk place setting, which she laid atop the white floor spread. With what ceremony she lit the candles! They would invite Mrs. Sobhani, who would come all the way from Moshir al-Saltana's clock tower to Shahreza Avenue hoping to partake in the blessings—she being a specialist in detailing the massacre and slaughter of the Imams and innocents and drawing tears from everyone. Batul Khanom was invited to most of these ceremonies. Sometimes Anis would forget to whom she was speaking and offer her advice. Opining that it was every believer's obligation to command the good and forbid the unlawful, she'd warn Batul Khanom against the stranger's glance and the fires of hell, urging her to wear at least a head scarf and commission a *sofra*, so that Abol-Fazl—may she be his sacrifice—would help to keep that American vamp away from Mr. Farzad. Little by little, Anis had stepped onto such a plane that no one could touch her. She believed she'd seen visions. Most nights she dreamed of Imams and saints. She wore a scowl, and seldom did her lips part in a smile. She whispered prayers and chants under her breath constantly. Batul Khanom was amazed at Anis's ingenuity in solving the women's problems, and at their belief in her.

But they jinxed Anis, that's for sure. One day, from morning to noon, Anis sat down to break up a loaf of sugar for the *rawza* that very day, a Tuesday afternoon. Mrs. Mirzapur had brought ice and rose water syrup. There were so many women packed into the reception room that if you dropped a needle it wouldn't hit the floor. But dear Hosayn Aqa did not show up to unfold the stories of woe and agony. As for the three gentlemen who were supposed to come to the *rawza*, two of them never did, and the third gave a perfunctory recitation, all the while with his eyes on the door, fidgeting every time the bell rang. The next day Mr. Mo'ini informed Batul Khanom that Hosayn Aqa had been picked up the day before in Rayy. He complained that now they might come for him, too—that, after a lifetime, Batul Khanom had gotten him into hot water. He said, "The man had distributed leaflets. After one of his well-attended *rawza*s he cursed the tyrant of the age and said other suspicious things." Batul Khanom asked anxiously, "What, for instance?"

"He said, 'O Imam of the Age, when will you show yourself? We're tired, we're fed up. Whoever has appeared on the scene has beaten us down. I'm tired. Come forth and take us into the shelter of your justice . . . I sleep in my clothes every night, lest I be unprepared when you come.' He said, 'On my way here this morning a young boy asked me, "Sir, will the Imam of the Age come by Friday?"'"

Batul Khanom asked, "What's suspicious about that? Aren't we all waiting for the Imam of the Age?"

Anis had her work cut out. Every day she'd make cutlets or vegetable omelettes, buy oranges and Turkish delight, and go from prison to prison, from Qezel Qal'eh to Qasr to Evin. She'd plead and beg, but there was no news of Hosayn Aqa. You'd think he had never existed. Women who shared her plight said, "Maybe he died under torture. Maybe they've done away with him completely, which is why they're trying to hush it up."

Early one morning a year later, the phone rang and a female voice said, "Batul, darling, hello!" The voice was familiar, but Batul Khanom was tired and had no mood or heart or interest or patience to rack her brains trying to recognize the voice. Retirement had proven tedious and her children had settled in America, never even writing letters. She asked, "Who's this?"

"My, my, Batul, darling, last year a friend, this year an acquaintance, next year a stranger. Don't you recognize your old friends anymore?"

Taken aback, Batul Khanom said, "Damn you, Anis! What kind of talk is that? I didn't recognize you."

Anis said, "Listen, sister, I wanted to invite you. Tomorrow's Friday. Please join us for lunch with Aqa. My husband, Mr. Barzanti, is sitting right here. Don't you say no now, not a word . . . if you love Mr. Farzad. All right? Give my best to Aqa; say Mr. Barzanti has invited him . . . "

Batul Khanom did not give her word, but took the address anyway: "Amiriyeh Street, Moniriyeh, opposite the bath . . . " The words came rapidly and precisely. Three quarters of an hour later Anis phoned again: "Dear lady, I implore you . . . I'm sorry, I spoke very badly. God damn me! I beg you by Miss Goli and Mr. Farzad's life, don't be upset. It was stupid of me to say I was Miss Goli's playmate and you were just like a mother to me . . . Come, dear Madam, come to the aid of this humble servant of yours."

Batul Khanom asked, "Where are you calling from?"

"This time from around the corner, Aqa Reza's shop. The guy is a big shot. If you don't show up tomorrow I'll really lose face."

Batul Khanom replied, "If I can persuade Aqa to come . . . "

But how could she persuade her husband to go to the house of a man they did not know? And what's more, for lunch? All afternoon she droned in his ear that once wasn't a thousand times, that it was a generous thing to do, that they should go see what Anis had gotten herself into this time. That night Aqa gave in. Next day, a bouquet of gladioli and tuberoses in hand, they honored Mr. and Mrs. Barzanti with a visit.

It was an old-style house, the pool surrounded by large pots of jasmine. On three sides of the garden were rooms, and from each emerged one or two people. Mr. Barzanti's sister was Heshmat al-Sadat, an old, hunchbacked woman with white hair and a very wrinkled face. Mr. Barzanti's two sons seemed like athletic, swashbuckling types. One of them was tall and unshaven. Laughing, Mr. Barzanti said, "May I introduce my eldest son, Tavilat." Mr. Barzanti's dentures were small and well aligned. Batul Khanom thought, Once I get to know him, I'll ask directions to his dentist. Mr. Barzanti was bald and made a smacking sound with his mouth, as though he were sucking hard candy and swallowing. Over his blue silk pajamas he had on a purple velvet dressing gown, and on his feet he wore maroon suede slippers. His daughters came forward one by one and shook hands. The first was fat, with long dark hair and a double chin. The second had plucked her eyebrows amateurishly. She wore a maroon blouse and beige skirt, and her stockings were the color of her blouse. Anis had the third daughter by the hand; she had frizzy hair and was wearing slacks. As for Anis, she wore a long-sleeved navy blue dress that fell below her knees and a floral head scarf. Her makeup was understated. She began to chatter easily: "How nice of you to come! You're very, very welcome." Letting go of the girl's hand, she took the flowers and said coyly, "May you be flowers yourselves, but may you live much longer."

Batul Khanom thought, What a sweet talker she's become!

They came to the reception room and sat on floral, velvet-upholstered sofas. The room looked like a pawn shop: pictures, vases, artificial flowers, tables, silver. Anis sat down and started off without any preliminaries. "Batul, darling, I wish you could have been there. Aqa and I went on the short pilgrimage this year. I stood under the golden eaves-trough and prayed for you and my dear Goli. I prayed so much that . . . "

She went and came back with the tea tray. Batul Khanom was suddenly the teacher again. She found out from Mr. Barzanti's boys that they were students, and the one whose name was Tavilat was a fourth-year architecture major. Anis said, "As if these strikes allow kids to study. Every day there's a strike. Poor darlings, they're home most of the time. I tell Aqa, 'Aqa, dear, bless your heart, send them both to America. I'll go along to settle them in and then come back.' "

Batul Khanom turned her attention to the girls. The fat one had failed the university entrance exam and now sat at home waiting for a husband. Anis crowed about her ostentatiously: "Lucky is the man who gets Monir al-Sadat. I don't want to jinx her, but she's perfect in every way." With a wink she asked, "Batul, dear, now that Mr. Farzad has finished his studies, when is he coming back?"

Batul Khanom laughed sardonically and said, "Farzad isn't coming, my dear. He's married an American."

Anis bit her lip. Looking at Tavilat, she asked, "What about Goli, darling? My playmate?" Batul Khanom's blood was boiling. She wanted to give Anis away, she wanted to give her a beating. She said coldly, "She isn't coming either. She's married."

"To an American?"

"No, no, an Iranian."

The girl in maroon blouse and stockings was a high school junior. Anis offered the opinion that no one could "write an essay better than Nayyer al-Sadat. She's written one on the White Revolution that makes your hair stand on end, you know . . . she got an A plus for it, you know."

Mr. Barzanti, lost in conversation with Batul Khanom's husband, turned to Anis and said, "Madam, how many times do I have to tell you? Don't say 'you know, you know' all the time."

"Whatever you say," Anis said. She turned to Nayyer al-Sadat and said, "Go get your essay and read it for our dear Batul. Batul is a teacher of literature."

Batul Khanom said, "Was."

Nayyer al-Sadat said, "How about after lunch, Mama?"

The girl with frizzy hair was a high school sophomore and apparently Anis's favorite. Anis asked Batul Khanom, "Do you know of a hairdresser who could straighten Monavvar's hair, you know . . . Monavvar's hair?"

Batul Khanom said, "No."

Anis expressed great displeasure with "these high school programs, really! They've confused both my child and the teachers. And I certainly don't have the education to help her. God bless my late parents, before I could know my right hand from my left they'd married me off. And the students wouldn't leave Haji Hosayn Aqa alone for a minute."

Mr. Barzanti was a retired employee of the Ministry of Finance. It was obvious that he was pleased as punch to find in Anis a domestic who served his ménage all day long and slept with him at night.

Anis laid out the spread on the floor in the guest room. Herbs, drained yogurt, jam, pickles, salad, *lavash* bread—everything was laid out symmetrically. She put out ten plates and brought in the food.

Mr. Barzanti said, "Madam here is an outstanding cook." Batul Khanom said, "Yes, we've had the pleasure." Then she added, "Many times." She wanted to say, For six years she let the cat steal and overcooked and undercooked and oversalted and undersalted and burned . . . it felt like she was eating straw. She vowed to herself never to mention Anis's name ever again.

Anis was doing all the serving and clearing. Neither the children nor the sister budged. As for Mr. Barzanti, he just watched. When she'd taken away all the lunch things, she brought in a brazier and put it in front of Heshmat al-Sadat. Then on a shiny tray she brought a kettle, a teapot, an opium pipe, and a tea canister. The tea canister was made of tin and had a picture of a man on a camel in a palm grove. The teapot was red porcelain. Mr. Barzanti said, "Please, have some." Batul Khanom's husband thanked him. Mr. Barzanti dragged himself toward the brazier, while Anis daintily spooned some tea into the pot and added boiling water from the kettle.

Brother and sister began smoking opium, offering it to each other and packing each other's pipes. Then Anis sat by the brazier and said, "With your permission." And Mr. Barzanti fixed a pipe for her.

The children went out one by one. Heshmat al-Sadat bade them farewell and said she was going to take a nap. Anis picked up the backgammon set from the table in the corner and put it in front of her husband. Mr. Barzanti and Batul Khanom's husband started a game, with Mr. Barzanti bragging. Batul Khanom thought she'd seen Mr. Barzanti somewhere. Suddenly it dawned on her: he looked like Aspirant Ghiyasabadi in the television series *My Uncle Napoleon*, but he wasn't as crafty.

نازایمان

# Childbirth

Just before sunset, the elder sister Akram returned exhausted from her clinic on the city's south side. She put her bag on the table in the hall. Mahin, who was sitting at the same table writing a letter, lifted her head and studied her sister's dusty and downcast face. "I'll be finished in a moment," she said. "Then we'll go for a walk." Zand Square, a public promenade, lay to the south of their house.

It was toward the end of the War, and their father had died recently. Mahin, who was studying at Tehran University, had not been present for his death and had grieved from afar. She had come to Shiraz to console herself by being with her family, especially since Tehran had become a frightful place. Unarmed soldiers, their collars unbuttoned, loitered everywhere, carrying their belongings in jerry cans. The bread in the city was hard as brick.

They walked toward the square. Facing their house was the army headquarters, with all of its lights on. "Why are they working so late at night?" Mahin asked.

Akram replied, "These are exceptional times." Then she added, "Brother should be coming home one of these days. I hope he comes soon. With things as they are, living in this house so far from the city without a man is very hard." Although Mahin had not complained about the condition of the house, Akram continued, "His orderly is very clever. When he comes, our lives will get much better." Mahin was still treated as a cherished guest, dear to her sister and mother, and she knew she would be especially well looked after.

Zand Square was dark except for a lone lamp in City Hall that lit a bright circle in the center of the square. Mahin observed Akram silently. She did not want to confront her sister about how exhausted she looked. It was Akram herself who began, "Aren't you going to ask what the matter is?"

"What is the matter?" Mahin said. And she thought, Perhaps you are in love, sister. It's about time. You're twenty-two, but you're so busy that you don't even find the time to think about love.

But in the dark Akram could not guess her sister's thoughts. "You know," she said, "since I've been back from Tehran I've been working non-stop. It's been almost a year now. But I should tell you: I regret having studied midwifery. As big as Shiraz is, there's only one midwife. Every time that I attend a childbirth, it's as if I am giving birth myself. I feel the pain with the woman, and we have no equipment. It's a shame."

"When you're tired, you start to hate your job. I think you should take a vacation."

Akram did not answer her, but continued, "Thank God, no one has died on me this past year. There's something to be said for that. I have only one patient who really worries me."

"What's wrong with her?"

"We are sworn to keep people's secrets."

Mahin persisted. "So don't tell me her name."

Akram said, "I'm tired and depressed. You're probably bored by now, anyway. How do you occupy yourself in a small town? This patient that I have keeps me very busy, but what keeps you occupied? All you can do is sit at home, and when the relatives visit you must take up mourning for Father all over again. And when you're so worn out from crying that you can't shed another tear, to have them all stare at you—"

"But I keep busy commiserating with you," Mahin said. "If you share your grief with someone, you feel better."

"I know, I know."

Mahin laughed and said, "Perhaps you are in love. You know, the most fascinating kind of pain is the pain of love."

"I don't know what you're talking about."

Mahin went on philosophically, "One who falls in love forgets all pain, fatigue, and depression."

Akram said, "Then you should open up a clinic and advertise: 'Nervous disorders treated with love.'"

"You can make fun of me, but the only fascinating gift of life is love."

"I'm not making fun of you," Akram said. "I just don't see love in as romantic a light as you do. I've seen love hanging from an umbilical cord; I've even sewn it up. I've seen love bleeding so that all the ergotamine in the world could not stop it. I've seen love in fear, fear of parents, fear of wife and child, fear of pregnancy. I've seen love in abortion. I've seen love in the knife that has gashed the thigh—all for a single glance from the gold-toothed beloved."

"Is this last case one of love bleeding? Which one of these is your patient in danger?"

Akram laughed. "You really want to know, don't you."

"Yes, very much."

"It's the case of love bleeding. She's a girl from a very old and respectable family. Whatever I do, her bleeding doesn't stop completely. I know for a fact that she's pregnant and I know that she has done something to herself. But she won't tell me a thing."

Mahin said, "Gain her trust somehow; tell her that her life is in danger. Ask her mother."

"She's terrified of her parents. If they suspect anything, they'll kill her. I've somehow made her understand, but she still insists that she is a virgin. She won't let me examine her."

"Send her to the hospital," Mahin said.

They turned toward home. In front of the army headquarters they saw a horseman, hunched over in the saddle. Their brother called them. They hurried toward him. He was wearing a turban and had wrapped himself in a military blanket. Mahin burst out laughing. "Why have you dressed yourself up like this? Perhaps you were traveling through Qashqai tribal lands and wanted to pass unrecognized."

They had not seen each other for three years. Mahin was wondering why he did not jump down from the horse and give her a hug. After all, she was still considered a guest in the house; every night, they cooked the dishes she had loved as a child.

Her brother said, "Don't tell anyone, but I caught malaria in Firuzabad and now I'm shaking like a willow. My head feels like it's about to burst. I left the soldiers with the corporal and took to the road on this horse. The poor creature is drenched in sweat." He laid his head on the horse's neck and kissed it. "I'll report at headquarters and then come home," he said. As the sisters started toward home, he called after them, "Don't tell Mother that I'm sick." He threw his turban to Mahin. As she unfolded it, she saw that it was his pajamas.

Akram said, "Don't touch it, it must have lice. I think he has typhus."

~~~ ~~~ ~~~

Mahin's eyelids had barely shut when the doorbell rang. They were ringing the bell and pounding on the door with the knocker, then with rocks and bricks. The knocking at the door mingled with the dog's barking.

Everyone was sleeping in the courtyard. Mahin grabbed her mother's *chador* from her bedside and, throwing it on her head, ran to the door. Mother sat up in bed and said, "Let me go. Don't trouble yourself. Dear me, my child is having such a hard time."

Mahin and the dog reached the door at the same time. Brother's horse was tethered to a stake near the door. A washtub full of barley and another full of water had been placed nearby. As Mahin walked by, the horse stamped its foot. When she opened the door, a coarse man tried to enter. "Don't move," she said, "or the dog will tear you into pieces." The lamp over the door cast a glow over him. What a brute he was! He was a giant of a man, with a felt hat and loose, baggy pants held up around his waist by a white string. She was about to ask him what he wanted when a woman wrapped in a *chador* came forward and began pleading, "I'm here to see Madam Doctor. I beg you, my daughter is dying. She's been writhing like a snake for three days now.

The village midwife has done everything she can. You can see the baby's arm." She banged her head against the doorframe.

Everyone was awake now. The light in the courtyard was on and Akram was unfastening the rollers in her hair. Mahin asked, "Are you going?"

"I have no choice."

Mother began to plead, "It's ten o'clock. There's a curfew; where are you going? Wait until morning. I'll be half dead with fear until you come back."

"Mother, I have to."

Mahin began to dress.

They set forth with the woman and the huge man. The descending moon stood watch in a star-speckled sky. Carrying her sister's bag, Mahin hurried along behind the three, who were walking briskly ahead on the gravel road. Except for the sound of their footsteps, nothing was heard. Though the curfew would not be in effect until midnight, there were no passersby; not even a bird was singing. Mahin was puzzled that they were heading north. Beyond their house were a few gardens, then the desert leading to the mountain. Mahin called to her sister. All three stopped and turned toward her when she asked, "Where is their house?" The woman answered, "Just before Bolverdi." Mahin said, "I hope you won't get us in trouble with the authorities." The woman said, "Bless you, dear, we're almost there. Madam here brings good luck. Just one push of her hand and the baby will be born. Then we'll return with you to your house and drop you off at your door, safe and sound."

≫~ ≫~ ≫~

They arrived out of breath. Drawing aside a sackcloth drape, they entered a small room, apparently the only room of the house. A smoky haze darkened the place. It looked more like a sheep pen than a room.

Several women sat on the floor, and Mahin could not tell which one was in labor. Half the floor was bare, the other half covered by a straw mat, and it was there that Akram found the future mother. The young woman was sitting, and her pallor was as yellow as turmeric. Her head hung to one side and her mouth was open. It was obvious that she could no longer keep herself upright, and she was swaying from side to side. Two women were holding her by the shoulders and supporting her back. "Say *'Ya Ali!'*" they kept telling her, but she wouldn't. She had no strength left.

On the mat in front of her lay a brick with a pair of eyes and eyebrows drawn in charcoal. The lips and cheeks were daubed in red. This hastily contrived puppet was supposed to trick the baby into coming out, to entice it to leave the darkness of the womb and enter the light of the world. Beside the brick was a brazier in which they had burned wild rue to keep the evil eye away. A woman was squatting in front of the woman in labor, holding out her hands in front of her as if she were about to take the child. As simple as that! Mahin observed the woman carefully. Her hands were big and dirty and her arms were bare to the elbows, revealing many strange tattoos. One was a lizard, or perhaps it was a scorpion. Her nails were tinted with henna and she wore an agate ring on her second finger. She was covered in a muslin *chador* and wore a black silk scarf bordered with green over her hair. She was calling out loud, "O Khizr, O Elias, deliver this child of God from that child of God."

This was all the effort she was making to bring out the baby, who did not want to come out and had kept so many waiting. One of those waiting, perhaps a sister or brother of the hoped-for arrival, had dozed off after the long wait and was sleeping on the mat behind the pregnant woman. Others were standing and doing nothing, merely staring dumbstruck.

Atop a wooden chest in a corner of the room, a tall oil lamp sputtered. Its glass casing was broken and patched with a piece of newspaper. On the single shelf sat a blackened skillet and a pitcher with a chipped mouth. The walls of the house were made of straw and clay and the ceiling was supported by beams, between which were spread straw mats. These were frayed and coming apart, but the clay was holding. Mahin saw her sister let go of the pregnant woman's hand. "She's been through hell," Akram said aloud. Turning to the other women, she ordered them out of the room and told them light the samovar. The women shuffled around, but did not go out. Suddenly a woman holding a Koran on her head appeared and said, "Bless you, my dear, what samovar?" Mahin took the pitcher from the shelf and Akram reached into her bag for soap. They opened the door and Akram threw the brick and the brazier out into the courtyard, which was filled with the voice of a man singing the Azan. Mahin poured the water while her sister washed her hands. Then Akram said to the woman holding the Koran, "Come on, get this child out of the way." The woman looked at the child asleep on the mat and replied, "My child will be cranky." Mahin picked up the child. A stinging alkaline smell made her feel sick. One of the women lifted the lamp from the wooden chest and Mahin practically dropped the child on it. The room was filled with every kind of smell, but it was the alkaline smell that made Mahin feel sick, not the smell of rotten meat, the smell of wild rue, the smell of the woman in labor, or the smells of tobacco and animal dung.

On the mat, Akram eased the pregnant woman onto her back. The village midwife could still be heard calling, "O Khizr, O Elias." To keep from retching, Mahin raised her head and tried to count the ceiling beams, but it was too dark.

Akram motioned to her to take the flashlight from her bag and shine it on the woman in labor. Akram had put on her gloves. The village midwife had gotten up and was leaning

against the wall. As Mahin turned her face away, still fighting
nausea, she caught the midwife's eyes, gleaming in the dark.
What a look it was! It was not the look of the old to the
young, nor that of the ignorant to the learned. It was the
look of the wolf to the young lamb. Akram was sweating.
She gave the woman an injection, and then, putting both
hands on her belly, pressed it with a twisting motion. The
woman's belly was trembling under her hands. Akram, now
wearing her white doctor's gown, was sitting almost between
the woman's open legs. Mahin had not seen her put the
gown on. She was just holding the light. A little bloody arm
was sticking out of a hairy cleft, from which blood was dripping. Mahin was seized with fear. The women were
whispering and the midwife droned on with her Khizr and
Elias. Mahin was afraid that the child might not arrive, and
they would have to stay until morning. She did not know
how her sister turned the baby. She was trying not to look.
She saw Akram push the arm in and turn it. Everyone,
including the woman with the Koran, was watching but
Mahin. Then the miracle. She did not know what her sister
had done. A tuft of black hair appeared from the cleft. It was
magic. Then Akram put her hands on the woman's stomach
again and pushed—how she pushed! She was sweating and
shouting: "Push, push, don't be afraid." No strength was left
in the woman, who said: "O saintly mother!" Akram said, "If
you don't push, it will suffocate."

The woman bit her lip. She wore patched-up brown stockings, pulled down around her ankles.

Suddenly Akram drew it out. She shook a long red chunk of meat over the belly of the mother, holding it by the feet. How ugly it was. The mother had raised her head from the mat and was watching. When the baby began crying, Akram placed him on the mother's belly. The mother laughed as if she had been tickled.

Akram stood, her gown bloody. Even Mahin's black dress was spattered with blood. Blood covered Akram's arms to her elbows. The woman holding the Koran came forward and kissed her hand.

When the job was done, Mahin took the pitcher again, but there was not a drop of water left. Akram asked, "Where can we wash our hands?" No one paid them any attention. The huge man who had come looking for a midwife had appeared in the room and was holding the baby, laughing and smiling at it. The women had gathered in a circle, leaning their heads together. Mahin was sure that they were conferring about her sister's fee. Apparently, the discussion centered on the village midwife, who was waving her hands angrily. Mahin thought, She shouldn't get anything. I won't let her. Finally, the woman with the Koran came to their rescue, saying they could wash their hands in the stream that ran by the front of the house. She no longer had the Koran on her head.

They stepped outside, so exhausted that they could hardly stay on their feet. After they had washed their hands and face, they felt a little refreshed. They could not tear themselves away from the cool, dark water. They sat by the stream, alone in an unfamiliar place. How happy Akram was! She was laughing. Mahin looked at the mountain, a monster pointed to the sky, which extended its hand in friendship. What was the fruit of their love, Mahin wondered, the stars that shine? The earth that brings forth the harvest? The trees that blossom? The water that murmurs in the stream? She asked Akram, who had bared her feet and put them in the water, "Did you see love?"

"Yes."

"How?"

"In the brazier full of wild rue, in the brick in front of the woman, love . . . "

Mahin stood up and said, "No. That's the viewpoint of a tired person. Even in that dirty sheep pen I saw love blossoming. I saw love in the smile of the mother when you put the baby on her belly. In the laughter of the man . . . "

When they tried to go back inside, they found the door shut. No one answered their knock. They knocked a second time, but still no answer came, as if all the people in the house had died. There was no sound and not even a light.

They took a stone and knocked, but the door remained shut. In the darkness of the early morning, fear filled their hearts. Akram shouted, "At least give back my medicine bag."

There was no answer.

"What use do you have for it?" Now she pleaded. "My pass is in the bag. At least give me that!" Silence again.

There was only the rattling of the door, echoing off the mountain. That was it. No one came to the door.

"She saved your daughter's life. Give back her bag!" Mahin shouted. She burst into tears, and was frightened by her own weeping. Akram pulled her close and said, "Leave them alone. They are very poor. Didn't you see the rags we used to swaddle the baby?"

They began to walk, their teeth chattering with fear. Then they began to run, skidding sometimes, losing their balance, but still running. They were running for their lives now. Akram was saying, "Don't worry, we'll be home soon." But she knew she was lying, and so did Mahin. Neither the stars, nor the stones, nor the telegraph poles, seemed to move. None of them offered any comfort. Out of breath, they sat on a rock. "There's no reason to be afraid," Akram said. "There's no one to be afraid of." Mahin said, "If that brute comes after us, I'll die of fear." Akram said, "Don't worry, he won't. Whatever we had, we left there. Why would he come after us?" Mahin said, "No, he will. He'll come to do us some mischief. I saw his eyes. They were gleaming like a vulture's."

Again they began to run. Only their footsteps sounded in the darkness. They had barely reached the first garden when a gruff voice commanded: "Freeze, don't make a move." Mahin said, "There you go, sister. He's after us. Didn't I tell you he'd come?" She sat on the ground. Akram stood by her side. A beam of light was trained on them. There were two men. Mahin shouted happily, "So it's you!" One was a policeman and the other an MP. The MP said, "All right, get moving. What have you been doing out at this time of night?" Akram said, "I'm the town midwife," and related the whole story. The MP said, "Then you must have an ID card. Where is it?"

"I told you, they took my bag, my flashlight, everything." The MP began to laugh, but the policeman was silent. They had reached their own house. "Here it is," Mahin said. "This is our house. You should know who we are. We are still in mourning—see, we're wearing black. Besides, our brother is an officer. Let us go, our mother might die from fright."

The MP said, "You can tell all this to the duty officer. It has nothing to do with me. I have orders to bring in anyone I see on the streets."

The policeman was hesitant, but he was afraid of the MP.

They passed the square, leaving behind the wide Zand Avenue with its closed shops. The policeman was silent, walking behind, but the MP, sometimes walking ahead of them, sometimes abreast of them, chattered continuously. "You're our third catch of the night," he said. "They'll keep you until morning." Then he became more familiar. "Come on, tell us where you've been. If you tell the truth, and there's a little something in it for us, I'll let you go." He winked. But the policeman, speaking for the first time, shouted at him, "You should be ashamed of yourself. Their late father, God bless him . . . "

"You mean they're telling the truth?"

"Of course they're telling the truth. Don't you see they're wearing black?"

"I know nothing about these things. They must have their IDs, or they have to clear everything in the station."

At the police station they were recognized immediately. The duty officer ordered tea for them, which never came, and when they told their story, he brought out his handkerchief and wiped tears from his eyes. He also slapped the MP, though Akram stopped him before he could strike again. Mahin thought, If I were the duty officer, I would kick the life out of him. She always talked of love, but at that moment her heart was utterly empty of love and compassion.

They were escorted home in a carriage. They walked in to find their mother sitting on the ground by the flower bed, weeping. Their brother was dressed and had tied their mother's *chador* around his head. He was saddling his horse.

When he saw them, he patted the horse's neck. Mother got to her feet and hugged them. How she wept!

Mahin had barely pulled the sheet over herself when the bell rang again. Brother's horse whinnied. The neighbor's roosters were crowing. Was it an untimely crowing, or had dawn arrived? And again there was the doorbell, ringing incessantly. She got herself to the door and opened it to a well-dressed woman, accompanied by a decent-looking servant, who was holding his hat in his hand. The woman greeted her and said, "We have come for Madam Doctor. We've come from Mr. ———'s house. Nasrin Khanom has started bleeding again and has become faint. She has lost so much blood that if you don't come, she'll give up the . . . "

# بی بی شهربانو

# Bibi Shahrbanu

They heaved and struggled to get their mother on board, but when the three of them finally made it up, there was no room for any of them to sit. More passengers were boarding the bus behind them, all calling, *"Ya Ali!"* The odor of sweat mingled with gasoline fumes. A soldier, fanning himself with his cap, sat to the driver's left. To the driver's right, a young man sat on a large drum.

Maryam looked at the passengers, most of them women holding fans in their hands. No one made a move to yield a seat, even to Maryam's mother. Maryam thought, Can't they see she's blind? She watched her mother standing quietly and gazing with open, unseeing eyes, as though straining to make sense of the hubbub. Standing in the middle of the bus in bewilderment, Maryam couldn't work up the courage to look anyone in the face. Just then, the driver's assistant shouted, "Move to the back!" Maryam took her mother's hand and pulled her to the rear of the bus. For a moment, she looked around and failed to spot her brother. When she did finally see him, sitting next to the young man on the drum, she was surprised—a pity she couldn't sit her mother down on the drum now.

The passengers hailed the Prophet and his household as the vehicle backed up and pulled away from the row of buses. Winding along several streets, it finally headed toward its destination on the road to the city of Rayy. Maryam was holding her mother's hand, feeling the weight of the bundle under her arm. Her *chador* was slipping from her head. She didn't know which to hold on to. She gripped the *chador* with her teeth. Every time the bus lurched, they lost their balance. Maryam was afraid they would both roll on the floor of the bus—if, indeed, there was any room for them to roll.

Once she was more or less resigned to their situation, Maryam caught the eye of an old woman who had apparently been watching them for quite a while. She was a bony woman, with a hump protruding from her *chador*. Maryam pleaded with her eyes; finally, the woman squirmed to the side. Crouching forward, she took Maryam's mother by the hand and sat her down beside herself. The young woman sitting on the other side of the old woman muttered, "Humph," under her breath and drew herself together. Taking the bundle from under her arm, Maryam put it on her mother's knees and grabbed hold of the metal bar. The breeze from the old woman's fan reached her. Gradually, her face opened up and she smiled at the old woman.

The young woman said, "To everyone else she's a mother, to me a stepmother."

"That's enough of that," said the old woman.

The setting sun appeared and disappeared through the unglassed, curtainless windows of the bus. The rocking of the bus and the heat, like an uncomfortable cradle, summoned Maryam to sleep. The women—who, like her, were standing in the aisle between the rows of seats and holding on to whatever they could find—blocked her view of her brother. Once when the bus lurched and the women swayed, she caught his profile. He was talking to the young man. What could he be talking about? she wondered. Her imagination took over: If I were him, I'd soften the guy up. Why, it's time for him to get married. He's got pretty good growth on his upper lip. I'd say, "Listen, friend. I have a sister who's very marriageable." No, that's a bad way to put it. I'd say, "I have a sister who can run an entire household. She's such a good cook it makes you drool. She irons suits like she's been doing it professionally. Besides, she's studied up to the fifth grade—history, geography, arithmetic." Then I'd say, "Hey brother, who manages for you? Who darns your socks?" No, that's no use either. He might say, "My mother" or "my sister." It's better if my brother says, "Brother, you and I better settle ourselves down. We should marry and think of getting our lives together." No, what a dummy I am! The young guy will give his sister to my brother and I'll be left holding the bag. He's more clever—older, too.

The bus rocked violently and all the passengers swayed. Maryam's mother almost fell out of her seat. But where could she fall? Her mother and the old woman had struck up a conversation. She heard the old woman reassuring her mother: "Why do you think so many people travel this way? It's not for nothing. Bibi Shahrbanu—bless her dear heart—has always come through." Her mother was saying, "If she grants my plea, if she restores my sight, I'll bring her a pair of silver eyes next year." Her mother's entreaty led Maryam along another path of fancy. Craning her neck to peer around the women, she looked at her brother, who was still in conversation. She thought, He's not thinking about *me*. Nobody says, "Look here, people, your daughter's ripe for marriage." They're all thinking about Mother. Can't really blame them, either. Am I myself any less concerned about her? Am I not her crutch? Didn't I leave school to take over the household chores, so Father wouldn't have reason to complain? Don't I slave and sweat from morning to night? Well, that's as it should be. Nothing frivolous about it. She's my mother, after all. I know my brother is talking about Mother. It was for him she went blind, anyway. He's probably saying, "I had an attack of trachoma and became an invalid. Couldn't go to the shoemaker's anymore. For all my mother's prayers and vows, for all the money she spent on doctors and medicine, I didn't recover. She'd bang her head against the wall, thump herself on the head, grab her breasts, and look up at the sky. She'd say, 'O God! Take my eyes and cure my son's.' She went blind first in the right eye, then in the left. She had a detached retina—a detached retina, and that's how we're all in this bind."

Maryam felt a tightening in her breast, a lump in her throat. She looked at her mother sitting sideways on the seat, her shriveled hands wrapped around the bar in front of her. Her open, lusterless eyes stared vacantly ahead, as though she was listening for something. Maryam cursed herself: Shame on you, you thoughtless girl! If you're married, who'll watch Mother? Who'll take her to the bath? Who'll watch the house so Father won't tear his hair out? Of course, it's only right for my brother to talk of Mother's handicap. What else? Besides, if the guy asked him for his sister's hand, he'd have to say, "Impossible! My sister should think of Mother." He mustn't allow . . . mustn't allow me to be married. My plea to Bibi was nothing but wishful thinking. How could I take such great misfortune to a husband's house?

Her mother's voice jolted her to reality. She was asking the old woman with amazement, "Did you say 'the Shah's daughter'?"

The old woman was saying, "What, you mean you didn't know Shahrbanu was the Shah's daughter?"

Her mother said, "No, how was I supposed to know? I never leave the house."

The old woman cleared her throat and said, "Yes, where was I? Right, Shahrbanu was the daughter of the Shah. She, bless her dear soul, is captured by the Arabs, who want to sell her in the bazaar in Syria. The Commander of the Faithful—bless him—gets wind of the fact that she's a princess. He entrusts her to Salman the Persian, and Salman gives her to Imam Hosayn."

The rest of what she said was drowned out by the clatter and din of the bus, which was now negotiating a bumpy road, rattling furiously. In the seat just ahead of the old woman, a baby was crying in its mother's arms, refusing to take the breast. The mother was at her wits' end. By her side several children of all ages and sizes were crammed together.

Maryam heard the voice of the young woman sitting beside the old woman. "No, no. Yazid was also a suitor of Shahrbanu's. But Shahrbanu marries Imam Hosayn. She sends Yazid a message saying, 'The world can be yours. I'm going to marry the Imam so that in the hereafter, in the day that lasts fifty thousand years, he can intercede for me and my people.'"

The old woman snapped, "Good Lord! Six of one and half a dozen of the other. Isn't that what I said? Seems like this pilgrimage is going to be ruined for me."

Maryam heard her mother interrupt them: "Dear lady, one must get along with the daughter-in-law, praise God."

The old woman continued to rage. "Lucky thing you're barren. What a hellcat you'd be if you had a baby!"

The young woman opened her mouth either to answer or to sigh—Maryam didn't know which. Whatever it was, the voice of the passengers drowned it out as they hailed the Prophet, and the bus, going downhill, gained momentum.

❧ ❧ ❧

Moaning and creaking, the bus pulled up at the bottom of the hill. Maryam and her mother were the last to disembark, following the crowd. One group of pilgrims, lanterns in hand, set off in search of a spot to spend the night. The soldier had put on his cap and was pumping a big kerosene lamp, while several women, wearing new black *chador*s, were standing smartly around him and covering their faces tightly.

Maryam's brother was carrying a large, dusty bedroll cover on his back. Maryam took his arm and squeezed it. "Look, brother, I think these ladies are nobility."

Her mother asked, "Sweetheart, what are they like?"

Maryam wanted to spare her mother the heartache; after all, her eyes were her mother's, too. "Their *chador*s are brand new. The soldier is carrying a big suitcase in one hand and a kerosene lamp in the other. One of them is very tall. In her *chador* she looks like a cypress tree."

Her brother asked, "Why'd they travel in this rattletrap?"

Maryam said, "Probably because they wanted to keep a low profile."

Mother said, "No, my love. The more one suffers on the road to pilgrimage, the greater the reward."

"What could these people want?" her brother said. "They have everything."

Maryam's little family had no lantern, but almost everyone else did. The soldier's kerosene lamp shone brightly amid the flickering lanterns of the others, which twinkled like indistinct stars, glowing one moment and fading the next. Maryam was constantly stopping and looking back, seeking someone with her eyes but never finding him. The last time she stopped, she made out the form of the old woman, their fellow traveler, in the light of the kerosene lamp. It seemed she was smiling and pointing at her.

Her brother lost patience. Pulling her by the hand, he said, "Keep walking. It's not good to be looking behind yourself."

"That hurt my hand. What's it to you, anyway?"

Mother began her usual sermon: "Maryam, whatever your brother says, say yes."

"But I said nothing. He just nags."

"A man's got to deal with a thousand worries," said the brother. "I really want Mother to get her sight back. I really want you to settle down. I'm tied down to you both. If I wasn't, by now I'd be as far away from here as India."

Mother said, "Say 'God willing.'"

Misfortune was engulfing them like black sludge. Struggling to stay afloat, they often collided, both hurting and comforting one another. Maryam felt so sorry for her brother she almost hugged him. To herself she said, He's thinking about me, too; yes, he is.

Her mother's voice caught her attention: "What a pity Reza can't come into the sanctuary. If he could, Bibi would grant him his wish, too. They say if a man approaches the sanctuary, he'll turn to stone. Then again, maybe that's all a lie."

"As for my wish, it's right here in my arm. How'd you like to see me enter the sanctuary and *not* turn to stone?"

Mother said, "Son, beg forgiveness. It's not good to doubt. I'll light a candle for you myself. They say a black man once doubted, but the moment he tried to enter the sanctuary he turned to stone. Don't make me sick with worry. Don't you take it into your head to enter the sanctuary, all right? Son, they say the mulberry tree near the cave entrance also grants wishes. I've brought along a bunch of prayer ribbons to tie to trees, for you, for your sister, and for your father. I've brought some for myself, too. But I'll say to Bibi, 'First grant my children's wishes, then heal my eyes. They're young; I'm a setting sun.'"

To distract her mother from reminiscing about her woes and desires, Maryam asked, "Mother, who told you all this?"

"The old woman sitting next to me said, 'In the cave there's a stream that flows into the Euphrates. Shahrbanu came out of this very cave to take to the mountains.'"

"By the way, what's the old woman come on pilgrimage for? How she nags her daughter-in-law! The daughter-in-law, too, how stiffly she talks . . . "

"You mustn't talk about others behind their backs. Are we short on sins ourselves that we should take on other people's as well?"

Maryam said, "I know why she's on pilgrimage. I was listening when she was talking to you. She's come so her daughter-in-law will get pregnant."

She desperately wanted to turn back and find the young man who had sat next to her brother in the bus. The youth was tanned and had dark eyes. He had broad shoulders that Maryam couldn't get off her mind.

They spread their things near a broad stream. First they spread their large bedroll cover on the ground, then laid a blanket on top. The air had gradually turned cooler. A mild breeze was blowing. The croaking of the frogs blended with more distant sounds. Every now and then, they heard the whoosh of a bird's wings. The other travelers, too, had spread their belongings at the edge of the stream. Some were performing ablutions and others were praying. Intermittent calls of "Allah-o Akbar" could be heard. The soldier's kerosene lamp was hanging from a tree and shedding a bright glow. The supposed women of nobility were sitting on a little rug. The soldier's collar was loose, and he was blowing on the samovar coals. His cap was also hanging from the tree. Maryam was sitting beside her mother on the blanket, facing the crowd, being her mother's eyes. No, this time she was her own eyes. This time she was looking for a lost one whom she could not find. Facing them, the woman with several children was spread out on the ground, suckling her baby, her breast exposed. Her husband, in shirt and drawers, was putting the family's things in order. The other children, who had been crammed together in the bus, were now milling about the mother. A young boy was helping his father pull out enamel plates from the folds of a faded blanket. Sometimes he would give a piece of bread to one of his siblings.

No, he was not among them.

Near the large family sat the old woman and her daughter-in-law, followed by the others. Last came the supposed women of nobility. Three of them had their backs to the crowd; the tall woman faced forward. He was not there, either. Maryam was anxious to tell Mother her secret before her brother returned. But what secret? A secret in whose blackness of misery she was lost. Maryam was looking for some connection between her lost one and the others. She looked at everyone again. But even the old woman and her daughter-in-law were strangers to her. As for *him* . . . it seemed she had known him for centuries.

Her brother finally came and they opened the food packages. In the darkness and stillness they fell to eating. Maryam was deep in thought, wishing she could ask, "Whatever happened to your traveling companion, brother? Has he sunk into the earth?"

A voice broke into Maryam's thoughts: "Bless you, dear, please help yourself. It's nothing, really."

It was the old woman with her love offering: two large chickpea patties on a piece of bread. She said, "We also have some freshly brewed tea. I'll bring you some if you like."

When they had finished dinner, the old woman came back with two glasses of tea and sat beside Maryam's mother and talked for quite a while. Maryam was happy that Mother had found someone to talk to. They were sitting in the dark, far from the other pilgrims. Or maybe they were not far, but they were strangers and alone. The mother's blindness had set her apart from everyone else, and even though her children were no longer children, they still lived in the shadow that had enveloped Mother—alone and in the dark, with a pain that stuck like a lump in their throats.

The old woman was speaking. Maryam could hear only her voice, occasionally a word or two. She was lost in her own thoughts. Uneasily, she scanned the crowd. If only she could find him. Suddenly her ears perked up at what the old woman was saying. Her heart pounded as she listened: "It'll be hilarious if he can't find donkeys. These prim and proper ladies, with all their airs—oh, won't they be put out! They'll have to sit on their rug till the crack of dawn."

Maryam joined the conversation: "So who are these people? How many hired hands do they have?" Her own voice surprised her, sounding as though it were coming from the bottom of a well.

The old woman said, "What do we poor folks know about the affairs of the great? Their husbands must be military officers; that's why there's an orderly with them. The young man who's supposed to bring their bedding is probably their servant."

Maryam had a lump in her throat, but she was about to laugh.

Rolling up her *chador*, she put it under her head and lay down next to her mother. Her brother was already sending up loud snores. Maryam knew she would have no sleep. Not only was her head not raised high enough, the ground under her was hard and damp. And besides the noise of the pilgrims and the light from their lanterns—more particularly, the soldier's kerosene lamp—the young man had also appeared, so Maryam's attention was fully drawn toward him. Lying with her back to her mother, her face to the crowd, Maryam was following the young man's every movement. She paid no heed to the large family eating their dinner, nor to the old woman and her daughter-in-law. All the pilgrims were before her eyes, but her mind was elsewhere. She saw only the young man as he pulled things out of a large suitcase. She saw him pumping the kerosene lamp, then spreading the ground cloth . . .

She was up so long that the lantern died out, followed by the other lamps. The family nearby simply lowered the wick in their lantern. Maryam didn't know where the young man was sleeping, but she knew it was not too far away. She fixed her eyes on the mother sleeping beside her infant, the suckling still holding her breast in its mouth. In the pale light of the lantern she saw the woman's colorless face and downcast eyes, seemingly watching her child. A fresh longing had lodged in Maryam's heart. No matter how long she pressed her eyes shut, sleep would not come. Despite her close proximity to her mother, she was far from her. She knew nothing of where she lay or what day it was. Every time she drifted into daydreaming, she remembered the first night her mother had gone blind—in the right eye, that is. Although she had still been able to see with her left eye, Maryam and

Reza had been overcome by bereavement, and for a while had not let on to their father. Her mind always went back to the day that she took leave of her classmates, the principal, the teachers, and the custodian and asked them to think kindly of her. That very night, her mother had lost sight in both eyes. Early in the evening, she had come out of the kitchen and suddenly plopped herself down at the edge of the pool and wailed pitifully. What wailing! She had neighed like a horse. What a cold night it had been! Maryam had realized that her mother was blind. Ah, misery! She remembered the day they had gone to the hospital and the doctor had said, "Old lady, you've come too late. There's no medicine now that can bring the light back to your eyes." And Maryam had burst into tears and her mother had said, "There's no escaping fate, is there?" She remembered they had hidden the tragedy from their aunt and uncle and cousin for a while. Every night the three of them would sit together and wait for Father. She and Reza would lean their heads together. Most nights they didn't even turn on the light. What good did light do? The stuff of her daydreams changed constantly. She always had pain in some part of her body that she couldn't pinpoint. But what devil had gotten into her skin tonight? What thoughts were running through her head? No matter how much she cursed and begged forgiveness, she couldn't get the tanned boy with large eyes and broad shoulders off her mind.

She saw herself suckling a baby, but her breasts were round and hard. She put her hands over her breasts and caressed them like two doves. Then her hands moved down; her body was soft and her hands were rough.

Then the young man was lying in place of her mother. What dark eyes! Maryam reproached herself: Girl, have some shame! Didn't you swear to serve your mother faithfully? Didn't you say, "I mustn't let her lift a finger"? Didn't you say to her, "Mother, I'm your two eyes"? Didn't you say all this? When Mother would come into the kitchen, stumbling and groping, and sit on the stool and ask, "How should I help you?", wouldn't tears flow from your eyes into the fire? Didn't she find out one day? Didn't she come and put her hand over your eyes? Didn't you put your arms around her neck? Didn't you say, "I'm your eyes"? Now you want to leave her and go away? How? That's ridiculous. Besides, nobody wants you.

But Maryam was sure there was someone who wanted her. Her whole body was overcome by longing. Her hands went to her breasts again. They were burning, and something under her left breast was beating fast . . . beating . . . she felt sorry for herself. Is it possible for Bibi to grant my wish and also cure my mother and also . . .

Gradually, her eyes grew heavier . . .

Maryam stood on a vast plain, surrounded by palm trees. As far as the eye could see, the plain was littered with the corpses of the slain. She was wandering among the dead. She did not know which one to look at. The blazing sun was beating into her head. The smell and the blood and the sight of the corpses and the sun turned her stomach. She was about to vomit. She wanted to run, to run fast, but she wasn't moving forward. In the distance, she saw a tent by a stream. The tent was red. A soldier stood guard at the flap. His armor was also red, and he held a long sword. The inside of the tent was murky. Suddenly, Maryam was standing next to the tent. The soldier was fanning himself with his hat.

A veiled woman riding a horse galloped by and, with a single leap, crossed the stream and landed on the other side. The horse had wings and was flying through the air. What a beautiful steed! But his mane was bloody. The woman was sitting upright on the horse, but she was wearing a veil.

Maryam knelt at the stream, but the stream was dry. She wanted to go back and ask the soldier for a bowl of water—she'd feel better if she drank. But the tent and the soldier were gone. The black-eyed youth appeared in the distance. He had a water flask on his shoulder and was dressed strangely, but his feet were bare. Maryam put her mouth to the flask and drank and drank. It was rose water syrup. "In remembrance of your thirsty lips, O Hosayn, father of Abdollah," she said. No matter how much she drank, her thirst was not quenched, and the flask ran dry. Maryam shook the empty flask in the air and gave it to the youth, saying, "God grant you water from the river of Paradise, young man."

Once again, she was near the tent. There seemed to be a fight going on inside. Men were arguing in a language that Maryam didn't know. Then the young man was sitting on two bundles of bedding on top of a donkey. He was coming from a distance. He was in the tent.

Maryam saw the veiled woman in the distance. Two young men were standing on the near side of the stream. They were in cashmere robes. They wore sheer veils over their faces, and also crowns on their heads. On the far side of the stream, two young men, similar in appearance to these two, were attending the veiled woman. No sooner did Maryam see the youths than she broke into a run. Before they could disappear, she was at their side, grabbing hold of the hem of one of their cashmere robes. The young man with a crown lifted his veil. It was the same young man with the black eyes. Maryam pleaded, "I'm lost, young man. This desert frightens me. For the love of God, young man, take me away from here." And the young man clasped Maryam by the waist and, in the blink of an eye, put her down on the other side of the stream under a large palm tree. But he himself vanished. His sweet odor had clung to Maryam's body. It smelled of the earth. Maryam had goose bumps on her waist where the young man had put his hands. She was weak in the knees. By God! What a tall, well-statured young man! What broad shoulders he had, what luxuriant growth on his upper lip!

Maryam was mounted on a horse with the veiled woman. They were riding tandem, Maryam sitting in front. The woman's arms passed under Maryam's breasts, and her hands were holding the reins. Maryam turned and looked at her. The woman, a full head taller than Maryam, raised her veil. Her face was so beautiful it glowed, like the orb of the sun— eyebrows joined together, eyes the shape of almonds, thin nose, small lips and teeth. Two angels in cashmere robes attended her. Both wore veils over their faces. One of the angels had luxuriant growth on his upper lip. It was visible under the veil.

The veiled woman turned to the angels. "Maryam is from the same town as I."

"We know, Princess."

Maryam asked the angels, "Did you say 'Princess'?"

"Yes, Princess. The King's daughter."

"I don't know what you mean."

The angel with the growth on his upper lip smiled. The other angel frowned. Maryam disliked the frowning angel. His cashmere robe was loose-fitting. It sagged on his body. His facial veil fell off constantly, and he kept pulling it back over his face.

They passed through strange lands, arid deserts and torrid wastelands, through various climes, the horse's hooves going clip-clop . . .

The angels were tired. They had taken off their crowns and were fanning themselves with them. The frowning angel no longer had a veil, and the pleasant angel had pushed his veil behind his head. Once, the pleasant angel's robe fell off his body. Maryam saw two pretty little wings sticking out from his back.

They reached mountainous terrain. There were mountains as far as the eye could see. Muddy water flowed through the valleys. The veiled woman dismissed the angels. She said, "We've arrived. You can go back. I know this area well." The angels took off their robes, shook them out, folded them, and tucked them under their arms. Flapping their wings, they flew away like pigeons.

Maryam wanted to talk to the veiled woman, but she couldn't get her voice out. She'd open her mouth, but no sound would escape through her lips.

Suddenly the veiled woman said, "I'm Shahrbanu."

Then it dawned on Maryam. She said aloud, "Dear me! I was looking for you. I'm so glad I found you. Grant me my wish. No, no, first cure my mother. I've brought you a pair of silver eyes. Where are they, now?" She reached into her bosom, but the silver eyes weren't there. Where had they fallen? Search as she might, Maryam couldn't find the eyes . . .

. . . It was a dark cave, and Maryam and the veiled woman were passing through it. A narrow stream flowed along the cave floor. The horse's hooves sank into the mud. The cave had no end. They kept going, and the cave was dark. Maryam was clinging to the horse's mane. She wanted to plead, but again no sound escaped her mouth. Shahrbanu said, "Get off. Go and look for the silver eyes."

They glimpsed light: red-armored riders, helmeted and booted, brandishing naked swords. They were laughing raucously. Maryam was no longer mounted. Shahrbanu prodded the horse with her knees and Maryam looked at her as she said, "O mountain, deliver me!" And the mountain before her yawned like a dragon and swallowed up Shahrbanu and her horse. Then, like a gate, the mountain closed behind her, but her floral *chador* was caught in the cracks. Her veil had fallen to the ground. The laughter of the red-armored riders echoed off the mountainside.

～～～

Maryam woke her mother for the morning prayer. She herself had been up for a long time. Maybe she hadn't slept at all. She wondered whether she had been dreaming or imagining things, or whether what she had seen had been in the twilight of sleep and wakefulness. Finally, she got up and took her mother to the stream to wash for prayers.

Maryam splashed water on her face and drank a handful, too. If it was a dream, she said to herself, then the horse's mane means a wish, and Bibi will definitely grant my mother's wishes.

Maryam had done her ablutions and was standing by the stream waiting for her mother when the young man, samovar in hand, came toward the stream. Maryam lost her presence of mind. She pulled her veil over her face. The young man sat at the stream's edge. Mother was standing, both hands outstretched. Maryam was looking at her; she was also looking at the young man as he washed the samovar. She didn't take her mother's hand. She was lost in wonder. Mother spoke up, "Maryam, dear, where are you?"

Maryam heard but said nothing. Mother's hands sought her veil first, then her hands. Mother said, "My dear, are you trembling because you're cold?" And they walked off.

They stood for prayer. But Maryam's mind was elsewhere. The ladies of nobility were also praying in their floral prayer *chador*s. The young man had put the samovar on the rug and the orderly was shutting the suitcase. Then something happened that made all the suppliants break off their prayers. Pandemonium had broken out. The father of the nearby family held a young boy in his arms, looking like a drowned rat, water dripping from his hair. The father brought the child and laid him down on the ground next to the mother, who was suckling an infant. Leaving the baby in her lap, the mother pounded her head with both hands. The children, of all sizes and ages, were scattered in the dirt around the father and mother. Some were crying, and some stared in shock. The woman was sobbing and pounding her head. The baby was crying, too. Maryam, her *chador* tied under her chin, went barefoot toward the child's mother and took the woman's hands. Maryam's mother groped and stumbled her way over to them. Maryam lifted the baby from the mother's lap. The baby was bawling in her arms and arching backwards. Maryam's mother sat on the dirt beside the woman. She asked, "What disaster has struck? Sister, what's the matter with you?" And she stroked the woman's neck and breast.

The woman said, weeping, "My child fell into the stream."

Maryam's mother asked, "Did anything happen to him?"

"He hasn't come to yet. I came on pilgrimage so Bibi wouldn't give me any more children, not so she'd take my child from me. God strike me dead! How ungrateful I've been! How I have tormented my child!" And again she burst into tears.

All the travelers were crowded around them. The tall woman lifted the child in the air by the feet. Then she laid him down and blew into his mouth. Again. Then she took the child's hands and repeatedly raised and lowered them. Maryam saw her eyes tearing up. The child stirred, and the tall woman said, "Thank you, God!"

Maryam's eyes were seeking someone and fell on her brother as he talked with the young man. She felt her anxiety returning. She squeezed the baby in her arms. What emotion had been awakened within her? It seemed as though someone else's child was the fruit of the tree of her own desire. The baby smelled of something besides milk; nonetheless, Maryam didn't want to be parted from it.

When things had settled down, Maryam spread the leftovers from dinner on the blanket so they could eat breakfast and go visit the shrine. She sat waiting for her mother and brother. Her mother was talking to the old woman, her brother to the young man. Maryam reached into her bosom and pulled out a green prayer bundle. She untied the green ribbon around it. Now she knew clearly what her wish would be. Her brother came and sat next to her. Then the old woman brought her mother. Mother's face looked more haggard than ever, as though it had been carved. She had turned ashen. Maryam asked, "Mother, what's wrong?"

Mother sat down and said as they ate, "Good God in Heaven above, what people these are!"

Maryam's brother asked, "Why? What's happened?"

"Nothing. The old woman, our fellow traveler, is asking for Maryam's hand."

Maryam's brother leapt for joy and asked, "Really? Does she have an unmarried son?"

"No, it's for the same son who's married. This wife can't have children."

"Meaning I should be his second wife?"

"Yes."

"No, mother, I'm not leaving you. I'm your eyes."

Maryam didn't know why she was suddenly happy. Mother sat up straight. Determination played in every wrinkle of her face. One might even think her eyes glowed with the spark of vision. She said, "Never. Never will I make my darling wretched." She seemed ready to go single-handed into battle against misery. She resembled a sleeping lioness who had raised her head but whose eyes had not yet adjusted to the light.

سُوتَرا

# *Sutra*

On my right sits Baba Zar, who is Baba Nuban, too. Beside
him are several large and small drums. My eyes are peering
at everything through a curtain of mist. It's a big crowd.
Apart from those sitting in a circle, there are others sitting
or standing here and there or coming and going. Somewhere they're roasting fish. The sound of the sea echoes in
my ears. I want to burst out crying. It's hot and muggy, and
my shirt is sticking to my body. It's always been this way, but
I first began to notice the weather after my motor launch
went down. Everything makes me sick to my stomach,
including the air. I wish the sun would let go of the tops of
the palm trees and go down. After all, it's left the blacks
alone. I'd like to sit in the shade of the blacks' shanties, one

awning on top of another. As though I were sitting under several awnings. Somewhere to be perfectly safe.

Baba Zar's hair, like all the blacks', is frizzy; it's turned white. That day, when I sought him out and poured out my heart to him, he looked me straight in the eye. I couldn't bear the pity, the loneliness, in his eyes. You'd think two onyx ring stones were set in his sockets.

"You've been possessed by the wind," he said. "You've become 'airy.' The conditions you describe are from Zar or Nuban. Your body was worn out. The wind is everywhere, at sea or on land. It's nested in your head. I'll start a performance for you."

Baba Zar calmly pounds the drums and the play begins. I, Captain Abdol, have apparently become Nuban's mount. This Nuban is usually caught by poor sailors, but right now I'm the poorest of the poor in the world. Or maybe I'm stricken with Zar. Baba Zar wants to bring down the rider and heal my wasted soul. I have come from Madras, but that seems like a thousand years ago. My friends say, "Captain Abdol is Indian and a Buddhist." Well, what's the difference? I belong everywhere and nowhere. And when it comes to faith, I accept all religions and believe in none. I hear my heart say, "Believe, believe." But reason admonishes me, "Listen, fool, and don't believe." My Indian friends say that only when Zar or Nuban, who have nested in my body like jinn, are overcome and my soul is set free, will I become one of the "airy" ones. As if I didn't have enough already! They say I'll let my soul out of the body and the spirit of Buddha will dwell therein. Buddha will speak through my tongue, and I will write his words with eyes closed. This will be his revelation, and revelation reaches the ear only when the ear has reached perfection. We'll have to see about that!

My enemies say, "Captain Abdol is a smuggler. He was a prisoner in Borazjan for a long time. He's abandoned his wife and child and now he screws around with Rostam."

Others say, "Oh, come on! Wasn't it Captain Abdol who scuffled with Jerry?"

Some ask, "Is it Captain Abdol you're talking about—that poet who's read as many books as he has hairs?"

In the Borazjan prison Taher Khan used to say, "What a voice you have! Soft as velvet. Give us another song so we can have a good time."

God pardon all those who are gone! God immerse Mr. Daneshmand also in His mercy! He took me into his school, taught me six classes, bought me books and pens and stationery, clothed me, gave me a roof to sleep under. I didn't want to bite the hand that fed me, but that's how I turned out. I got bored. What was I to do? I like to throw caution to the winds and seek excitement.

For many years now I've been wandering from coast to coast. Land depresses me; I find peace at sea. I know so many coasts and ports like the palm of my hand. Bandar Abbas was my second home. And Hormuz, Qeshm, Hengam, Kharg, Kong—there's no port in the southern seas in whose waters I haven't cast my anchor. How many times do you suppose I've been to Bombay? And what about Calcutta, Jedda, and all the other cities and ports whose names I've forgotten? I can navigate the Gulf, the Arabian Sea, the Indian Ocean, and the Aden Strait with my eyes closed. They used to say, "Captain Abdol has a mermaid for a wife who guides him through the seas." But I had a compass in my pocket, which I would take out in storms. Now that I have found this mermaid wife, everyone says I'm a crackpot. Baba Zar says I'm "airy."

The drums beat faster. They're singing. I want to burst into song myself. To sing only for Taher Khan, and for him to lower his head and say, "Oh my, oh my! What language are the words? Arabic? Swahili?" My heart sinks. To myself I say, Get up, start running and throw yourself into the sea; get up and go into the desert and cry out. Baba Zar looks at me, as though he's telling me with his eyes, "Be patient."

I sway to the rhythm of the drum. I was moving and didn't know it. To my left, to my right, men and women are moving around me like clock pendulums.

The sun disappeared a while ago. There's a murmur in the palm trees and the blacks' shanties. Somewhere they've built an oven and are baking bread. Where's the wheat?

Who's the master of bread and salt? Where are the greetings? The cows and the sheep grazed on the unripened wheat. But where are the cows? Where are the sheep? They died of thirst. Where was this? I think it was Hormuz. People bought fresh water at four *rial*s a pail. For several days water hadn't been delivered, and the children and the grown-ups were thirsty. They'd lower a piece of felt to the bottom of a well that had a spot of water. When it was wet, they'd pull it up and suck on it. The wheat in the storehouses was attacked by vermin, rotted, and became fodder for the mice. I saw people, each holding one sack, descending the road that leads from the fortress to the city. On the Bandar Abbas pier, trucks unload the wheat from ships, which have come from the other side of the world. Then the trucks move, and as they shake wheat starts spilling out on both sides of the road. Women and children sweep it up with brooms and dustpans and pour it into sacks and take it home to make bread. The man of the house has returned, having caught some fish in the sea. I really want some black tuna, but the fish only surfaces on full-moon nights. The tuna stares at the moon, and gazing at the full moon costs it its life. But what's in its life other than this gazing?

The beat of the drums and the words they're singing carry my thoughts to a thousand places. I've gazed on many things. The world has a great deal to marvel at. But that mermaid who held my hand and took me to her house at the bottom of the sea was the most marvelous of all. Get up, boy! Pluck a bunch of dates from the sayyid's palm tree given to charity. We have a guest. It's Captain Abdol sitting in the shack. The kettle has come to a boil and the tea is brewed. Three walls of the shack are made of straw curtains sewn together. The fourth is a collection of oil cans piled on top of one another. There is a dead tree in the corner and they've tied a clothesline to it. I don't know where they've tied the other end. My clothes have dried. The woman is patching up the holes. She's even smaller than my daughter. Her newborn is sleeping on the ground, and the other kids are milling about. Flies are swarming. Everything looks black under the coating of flies. At sea you won't see even a single fly . . . so immaculate. They're grinding the wheat picked up from the road. I don't see the mill . . . Beneath the millstone of life, it is I who have been crushed. It seems I'm still floating, lost at sea on a bale of cotton. My launch was the bride of the seas. She was the desire of the nights and days of my youth. I gave all my life's savings and bought her in Kong from Jaber the sailor. Her wood had come from far away, from Africa, from India, from I don't know what corner of the world. Was it teak? Was it rosewood? I don't know what kind of wood it was that made your heart skip a beat when you rubbed your hand over it. To me it was sweeter than sandalwood and ebony. I'd press my face against the wooden hull of my launch and imagine that once upon a time I had been incarnated in this world as sandal-wood. I'd polish my launch with shark liver oil until she sparkled. They'd mounted a diesel engine in her, and when it started it sounded like a human heart. Whenever we came in from the sea, Rostam and I would fall to polishing the launch from end to end so she wouldn't crack. I'd bought the shark liver oil from Jaber the sailor.

Rostam would say, "Captain, I think this is whale oil."

I'd say, "Boy, how would you know?" He would laugh.

The captain's cabin looked out to the sea, and I'd scan the water to the horizon with my binoculars. How many icons and statues I had bought from every city and port! Hindu gods, statues of Buddha, the face of Ali, Jesus on the cross, Moses grazing his flock, King Solomon on his throne. I looked far and wide for an icon of Elias, but no one has drawn his picture yet. Elias is alive and present in the world. If you see a man without a shadow, cling to his robe, for that is Elias himself. He's a stranger come in from the sea. As soon as he steps ashore, the earth opens up and he plunges into the chasm, as if going home. All the fishermen have seen him. At night he comes out. How many times have I gone to the shrine of Bibi Ayesha on pilgrimage! I know she was a pretty woman, nicely done up. At sea she got sick. They wrapped her in a blanket and threw her overboard. Her corpse washed ashore. If you have a lost one, go to her shrine. I went, too, and asked her for my lost one, the mermaid. I had bought all kinds of statues of the Buddha. I liked his smile. His smile said, "I know all the secrets of the world." Dear God! How can a man be so calm in such a world and smile, too?

In my cabin I'd look at the icons and statues, and Rostam would bring me tea. His eyes were the color of charcoal, his face the color of sandalwood, and the fire in his eyes told you, "I'm young, I'm strong of arm, and I won't buckle under." And you'd believe it.

It was Friday when I prayed with the old salts. There were nine of us, and we had twelve passengers whom I was smuggling into Dubai. All of them had forsaken everything they had. Their hopes had been dashed, and Dubai twinkled at them from afar like a star of hope. The glow had bewitched them, and they were setting out to grasp it. Perhaps the twinkling was fate.

I shoved off from the pier at Bandar Abbas at two in the afternoon. Our cargo was a few sacks of eggplant and vegetables, twenty bales of cotton, and several baskets of dried dates. We reached Qeshm at three, taking on another passenger with five cans of kerosene.

Through my binoculars I could see the ship *Dara*. She seemed half burned. They were towing her into Qeshm. I guessed the *Dara* had been bound for Dubai, too. I steered the launch to pass her by . . . I don't know what happened—the sun blinded my eyes so that I couldn't see, or I wasn't paying attention . . . we collided. A plank on the side of my launch was stove in, and another on the bottom. My launch had been holed! Seamen and passengers alike set to bailing, returning the water to the sea in buckets. But what was the use? The sea had sought out the holes and was rushing in like a rampaging lunatic. A few passengers were retching. Two lay on the deck as water flowed over them.

My launch was everything to me. She glided over the seas like a bride, and the waves kissed her. My house, my country, everything I had to my name; my wife, my mother, my daughter—my launch was all of them. I told Rostam, "What are you waiting for? Break up the planks and give them to the passengers. Toss the bales of cotton into the sea . . . "

They saw that the launch was listing, sinking . . .

Where is my wife? Whatever happened to my daughter?

In those days, Zahiriyeh had been a red-light district. I'd sit behind the counter myself and take the money. I wasn't thirty yet. It was out of loneliness and homesickness that I got married so early. I myself would throw my wife and daughter into the arms of the sailors from faraway places. Early on, my daughter would cry and say, "Daddy, it hurts!" After all, she had just turned eleven. An Italian sailor deflowered her. That night I did not sleep at all. Outside the nuptial chamber, which was really no nuptial chamber, I paced up and down and smoked. My daughter shrieked twice or three times and I heard her crying. I went in. She said, "Daddy, that hurt so much." The Italian sailor was young, too, pretty much a child. He was sitting on the floor, his head on his knees, still naked. I took my daughter in my arms and laid her head on my chest and put her to sleep. I remember singing her a lullaby. Even in sleep she was sobbing. The next few nights, whenever a customer would come wanting her, she'd start to cry. I'd yell at her; once I even beat her. She sagged onto the floor and just sat there. Every time my wife went off with a customer, she'd fix her eyes on me, like a lamb being watered before the slaughter. There was no reproach in her glance. I wish there had been.

Once she said, "Man, you're a man of the sea. The sea is generous—it'll provide for us."

But I needed money to buy a big boat, then an old launch, and finally go to see Jaber the sailor in Kong.

That day when the Arab came for the second time, he had bought a golden anklet and veil for my daughter. She put the veil on her face, saying, "Look, Daddy, isn't it pretty?"

My daughter was lost. I left the bordello. I abandoned my wife, Tavus. I had bought her ten gold bracelets and a contraband watch, a box of contraband fragrant tea, and a contraband red leopard-skin blanket . . . besides, she had a bedroll to earn her living. That bed smelled of men of the sea. It had been a long time since I had even touched her. Tavus stared at me again like the lamb going to the slaughter. Don't tell me the lamb doesn't know she's being taken to be slaughtered. She's not blind; she sees the knife in the butcher's hand. And if she doesn't understand, so be it. Perhaps Tavus didn't understand, after all. My eyes teared up, but I betrayed nothing. I said, "Good-bye." That was all.

When I boarded the ship with my father in Madras, no matter how I pleaded, he wouldn't let me bring my monkey. "Be grateful I'm taking you," my father said. My monkey made a leap and reached the boat. My father chased him. My monkey climbed to the top of the mast and sat in the crow's nest. The skipper swore. My father climbed up the mast, tucked him under his arm, and brought him down. The skipper ordered the monkey to be put ashore. I wept. My father said, "I'll tell them to put you ashore, too." Where's my monkey now? Forty, fifty—I don't know how many years. He can't have stayed alive all this time.

I bought a suitcase. I used to steal across the border into Kuwait, bringing back goods and selling them at the Misfits' Bazaar at the corner. Watches, rolls of fabric for men and women, tea, toys, umbrellas, blankets . . . Goddamn greed! I took to smuggling the white powder. I devised places for the stuff in my suitcase, filling the rest of it with junk that the wives of the navy officers in the fortress killed for.

The drumbeats slow down. The singers fall silent. I begin to move slowly. The crescent moon is hanging by the top of a palm tree . . . I smell blood. A basin full of blood sits in the middle of the circle. Someone says, "Drink." I can't. I'm sick. The drums die down. A woman wearing a black veil gives me a loaf of bread with a few dates and a piece of roasted fish. Everyone is eating, but I can't. I want to rehash my life and find out where things went awry. From what I know, it seems all wrong. What could Baba Zar do? I was thinking of him, but he snapped me out of it. I saw my life, and the review calmed me. Someone gives me a bowl of water. The water smells of moss. I drink, and it cools my burning heart. They bring a standing lamp and place it near the basin of blood.

I'd take the white powder to sell it at our white temple in Bandar Abbas. The young guys would come and buy the stuff and snort it greedily. Right there. Now our temple is in ruins; not that it was thriving very much in those days, either. The inside is filthy. Once—only once—I felt inspired to pledge to renovate our temple. But when I really thought about it, I saw that no temple can come close to the human heart, and the heart can't be renovated. I wish it could. I was in love with the sea. He who knows the sea gets restless on land. He's like a fish fallen on the sand, burning for the sea.

Four years of my life passed in the prison of Borazjan. I put my money on the table and told them with perfect frankness that I had no one to come for me. They felt pity. Taking their due, they gave back the rest of my money. First I got acquainted with Sayyid Mohammad. He taught me the how-to's of prayer. He was a youngster who had shot dead a gendarme and crippled a policeman. He'd say, "Retribution for my father's blood." He'd say, "The policeman is still deformed in the neck and won't drop charges." He was a lifer. I became friends with him and wanted to take things somewhat farther. He wouldn't. There's no one quite like Rostam.

Two months later I came to know Taher Khan. He was in another part of the prison. He was the kind of man that if there were a thousand like him, the world would be a lovely place. Taher Khan opened my eyes and ears. He gave me his books, and I read them and wondered to myself, How delightful reading books can be! And I've been ignorant of it. He'd call all the jailbirds together at night and read to them. He'd give us all lessons. When he got tired, I'd raise my voice and sing a folk song. Even the guards would come and listen. Taher Khan didn't like folk dances. He'd say, "There's too much shaking and jiggling." After I danced for him a few times and saw that he didn't enjoy it, I stopped.

Despairing of the sayyid, I spent most of my time with Taher Khan. With him I had a different view of life. I wanted to put my hand to something in the world so they'd write my story. I served him openly and unashamedly. I wanted to make him fish fricassee, but I couldn't get the utensils. I swept his room and shook out his blanket, which I washed twice. I did this so he'd show me his world. I was happy to die to bring a smile to his lips. But how could he smile? Once I kissed his hand and said, "I'll do whatever you say." He said, "I'm no lord and master."

Suddenly they begin beating the drums again, and my heart sinks. The singing roars in the wilderness and the plain and over the sea. All the terrors of life are massed in my soul. My legs are numb, ice cold, and I have gooseflesh all over. A tremendous dread . . . Good God! What is this fear that has beset me? Don't we all end up dead anyway? And as Taher Khan says, death overtakes everyone, so what's the fear?

One morning I took Taher Khan some tea. I saw he was sitting up in bed, resting his chin on his hands. "Didn't you pray today?" I asked. "No," he said, "last night I saw Majid and Masud in a dream, in the house they grew up in. I woke up at prayer time, but shut my eyes again so I might dream of them again. They toppled my two cypress trees, felled them in the dust." I said, "Taher Khan, didn't you always say, 'God gives and God takes away'?" He said, "That last day that I went to the prison to see my boys—they'd given me visiting time—was the last day my boys spent in this world. The heat was enough to drive you crazy, but Majid was wearing a jacket and his hands were in his pockets. His friends later said that they'd torn out my boy's nails and that he hadn't wanted me to see them . . . but Masud had been so badly tortured that he was crawling on his hands and knees. I didn't get to see my Masud one last time."

To take his mind off his boys I said, "Taher Khan, you've never told me what you're in prison for." He said nothing. Moments went by. Finally he spoke. "The Kurds have a very good saying. They say, 'Let the water carry you away before you cross the coward's bridge. Let the lion tear you apart before you lie under the fox's shadow.' The man who tore me apart wasn't a lion, though. He was a puppet in a puppet show."

I said, "There's a similar saying in Bandar Abbas. We say, 'Don't walk with the coward or you'll turn yellow.' We say, 'Don't eat at the tyrant's table, for going hungry is a hundred times more honorable.'" I said, "Taher Khan, carrying the camel's load isn't hard, but being under obligation to a coward is."

Taher Khan got up from his bed and said, "God bless you. You've made me feel better."

I don't want to think of Taher Khan and his sons. It gets me badly riled up and I lose my cool. I've been this way for a long time. My heart pounds so it reverberates through my chest and screams in my ear. I get anxious, and I start to think sea sprites hold my reins. This affliction of Zar that they say I've caught must be one of the sea jinn . . . when I close my eyes at night, no matter how hard I press the lids down, I can't sleep. When my daughter was little, I used to sit cross-legged and put her to sleep on my lap. I'd tell her stories of the seas; I'd talk about my monkey and about my father, who was swallowed up by the sea. I'd tell my daughter, "Close your eyes or sleep will tiptoe into them, and I won't be able to take it out." I'd say, "Close your mouth now or the mice will come and chew your teeth."

One day I took her to see a little ship that had run aground in the old Bandar Abbas harbor. Where had the ship come from? I didn't know. When? I didn't know. What had happened to the passengers? I didn't know.

How many seamen in that ship had been stricken by Zar or Nuban? Moss had covered the rusty ship from end to end. There was another rusting ship by the stone embankment at the shore. She stood in the captain's room in the first ship and said, "Daddy, this ship is a house for jinn, isn't it?" Then she ran over the narrow rivulets the waves had left on the shore and said, "The jinn come this way and go to their houses. They go to the sea in the day, and at night they return to the shore to sleep. Poor things! I hope they close their eyes at night so sleep doesn't get into their eyes. Isn't that right, Daddy?" I said: "No, my dear. These rivulets are the footprints of the waves so their return to the sea will be easy and they won't get lost." Suddenly they pound the big drum heavily and my heart jumps and I move to the right and to the left. Heaven forbid if the jinni of Zar has traveled down the same rivulets and made its home in my body . . .

Mr. Daneshmand got me a birth certificate. He picked me up from the streets and alleyways and gave me the name Abdollah. My birth certificate says I'm fifty-eight. My hair has turned white as flour in the mill of life, my whiskers salt and pepper. I remember my childhood name—it was Muraji. I remembered my monkey, too. I have vivid memories of my mother. She was a deep dark complexion and wore a tattered sari and her breasts were exposed and her protruding ribs were also visible. But she had large, dark eyes. I've got her eyes. I saw myself in their pupils and I threw my arms around her and laughed. But laughter wouldn't come to her lips. In one of my journeys I went to Madras and looked for her high and low, but didn't find her. At night I went to see the movie *Mother India;* Nargis was in it. I wept and wept. How many Indian films I've seen!

At night my mother, my monkey, and I would sleep in the crowd in the large square. I remember we had an empty can. I'd go fill it with water from the fountain in the middle of the square. Sometimes I'd stand in my rags under the fountains and get wet, but when the infernal wind hit me my clothes would dry on my body. The doorman at the hotel would come and empty the table scraps in a big green box. We'd descend on it—men, women, children—and get into fights. I almost got trampled in the crowd. But I was nimble and would get a few pieces of bread, a leg of chicken, or a couple of bananas. I'd give my monkey a banana. He was a thief; whenever I returned empty-handed, he'd scoot away to steal something, finding his way into the hotel kitchen. Sometimes he'd beg, putting one hand over his eyes and holding the other one out to passersby. We slept on the ground. As we slept, cows walked unhurriedly over us. One night a cow pissed on me. My mother held her hands together under the urine to fill them and splashed it on her face and mine. My father had gone to sea and my mother was praying that he'd come back with his hands full.

My father and I were standing at the shore. My mother was wailing. When I left Tavus, she had a look exactly like my mother's. Now I understand that in both their eyes helplessness was flickering.

When the launch sank I heard my mother's wailing. What became of the passengers and the twinkling of their star of hope? How did the sailors end up? God is all-great! Great is the God of Abraham! I heard these cries for a long time. Did they all last for a few hours on the cotton bales? Did the boatmen notice them and gather them up? How about the men who were towing the *Dara?*

On a cotton bale, I was grappling with the waves, bobbing up, bobbing down. It was a wreck of a boat, and I, a seaman who'd washed his hands of life, knew full well that when the cotton became waterlogged it would sink to the depths. Where was the shore? No star shone above my head. I sank into one eddy, then another. The sky was dressed in black; no anklet of the crescent moon, no glittering coins of the stars, no starry way to Mecca, no way to our temple in the port could I see. Once—only once—I'd made a vow that if I got rich I'd clean our temple and refurbish it. But what was the use of a temple in which no one circumambulated and which the gods had abandoned? I wanted to offer incense and flowers at the feet of the idol, but it was broken into pieces. Whatever relates to God must be in a clean place, in good weather. It's not for nothing that God is in the skies. It's not for nothing that prophets go to the mountains and converse with Him. Clean, unpolluted air is a necessity of the soul.

I asked Elias for help. I invoked Buddha, remembered Mohammad, Jesus, Moses, Ali, Abol-Fazl, and Hosayn. I summoned to my aid the spirits of the seventy-two—the seventy-two men the sea had devoured in one swallow in the gulf the people had named "The Spirits of Seventy-Two." Bibi Ayesha's tree of desire, and Sindbad the sailor's, and Mir Mohanna Daghabi's, and Jaber the sailor's . . . Jaber the sailor must be a descendant of Sindbad the sailor; he it is who had made my launch. I wish I had pulled out my compass. It was in the pocket of my jacket. Rostam hung the jacket from the peg and brought me tea. I said, "Rostam, we'll take the dates to Madras. If we don't find buyers we'll take them to . . . "

The sea water was salty and I was thirsty. I was so cold. The wind blew from the land, pushing me farther and farther seaward. I was so far from land that I knew my corpse wouldn't even wash ashore and I'd have no grave. Like the desert, the sea was cleft by the rising and falling of the waves, pulling me to the bottom. I wept aloud. Who had ever seen Captain Abdol cry until then?

I pull my handkerchief out of my pocket to wipe away a tear. I stop moving for a moment and look at Baba Zar. Have I been afflicted with the Zar or Nuban, or with the madness of the whole world?

I move my head to the left and right, and my body follows the movement of my head. I have become calmer, even though the drums beat faster and the singing reciprocates the terror of the night.

I reached with my hand and took hold of the mermaid's tresses. I came away with a fistful of hair. If the mermaid didn't exist, why did I have a handful of black hair in my hand when I washed ashore?

The mermaid took my hand and led me away. We left the darkness of the sea behind us. The lower depths were bright and warm. I hadn't kissed a woman for a long time. She laughed when I kissed her. Her teeth were white as pearls, her lips salty and hot. A school of parti-colored fish, scales glittering with a thousand colors, danced around us. A golden fish rubbed its face against the mermaid's scales. The mermaid asked, "Have you studied your astronomy?" The golden fish answered, "No, last night the stars did not come out. We studied geography." I laughed. A tuna emerged from among the other fish and said, "Mermaid, dear, I listened to the stars last night. They said to each other, 'And tomorrow night? Shall we come out, or lie in ambush behind the clouds like tonight?'" The mermaid asked, "Have you seen my brothers?" and the golden fish said, "Early this morning they went hunting. A shark has been sighted near here."

We went on and on until we reached the mermaid's house. Her gardens were planted with white and purple coral. Colorful fish were dancing there. Some had striped scales that emitted light. These provided lighting for the house. In the mermaid's bedroom, a few of these fish kept guard. Her bed was an enormous oyster shell. I saw her face. Her eyes glowed with the radiance of all the diamonds in the world, or perhaps the light from the glowing fish was reflected in her eyes. In the smile of her lips and the sparkle of her pearl-white teeth was an expression that I had sometimes seen in Rostam.

Rostam lived with me from the time he was a child—the same time that I had vowed to devote my life to the sea. I had bought an old launch. Rostam's father gave me his hand and said, "Sold, for one hundred *tumans*." "Done," I said. His father said, "I wish you joy of him." Rostam cried. He asked,

"What are you going to do to me now? Cut my head off?" I didn't touch him for a while. Once he was housebroken . . .

With every moment, the mermaid's eyes flashed like those of someone I knew: like the eyes of my wife, Tavus; like those of the woman wailing on the beach in Madras; like those of my lost daughter; like those of Rostam and Mr. Daneshmand and Taher Khan. Her eyes showed more intelligence than sorrow, more understanding than reproach. When she spoke, I became calm. When she told me stories, I forgot myself. My daughter put on the anklet and wore the golden veil and asked, "Daddy, aren't they pretty?"

I felt the mermaid's body and smelled her. She smelled of the sea at dawn. She didn't smell of the sea's menstruating. I know all the smells of the sea. Which is the sea, man or woman? If it isn't a woman, why does it menstruate? When the sea creatures die, the sea takes this smell.

The mermaid was covered in shiny scales, like the dress that the Arab dancer in Aden had worn when the men were cheering, but my eyes were on the door, waiting for Rostam to come. When you stroked her scales in the right direction, they were so soft. I wanted to make fish fricassee for her, if only I could get hold of garlic and tarragon and coriander. But she would not touch fish. They were relatives. She ate seaweed, which her relatives picked and brought her in a flash from any corner of the ocean floor. She ate it absolutely raw. I ate it, too—it was delicious, every conceivable kind of green, tasting like lettuce or baby radishes.

She pleaded with me: "Marry me, before my brothers come." I said, "I'm not one for marriage and that sort of thing. The sea is my wife and child, and Rostam is the source of my delight." "That's fine," she said. She put her emerald ring on my finger. Here it is, still on my finger. Whatever became of her hair, which was in my hand? No one believes that she gave me her ring, that her hair was in my hand. They tell me, "There was a bunch of seaweed in your hand." They say, "You don't remember, but you yourself said that you were looking for your mother in Madras and you had bought this ring to put on her finger," and, "You haven't seen a mermaid. Maybe you fell asleep and dreamed of her. Maybe you're crazy and hallucinated and took it for real."

In the prison of Borazjan, Taher Khan used to say, "Illusions, dreams, and visions are all aspects of reality. Even the reflection that you see of yourself in the mirror is a form of reality." The doctor in Shiraz used to say, "Captain, you had a bad fright. Be thankful you found a plank by chance and managed to get yourself to shore." However many times I swore that the mermaid had given me the plank so I could escape her brothers' clutches, the doctor didn't believe me. He wrote me a prescription; some of the medicine couldn't be found. I don't know why the doctor, the exorcist, and all my friends were trying to take away the greatest pleasure I had ever enjoyed in my life. If I had met a mermaid, a sympathetic, kind, understanding, cheerful woman who never nagged, whose welfare I was careful to safeguard, neither of us wanting to make a slave of the other—what offense could this do in the world and what harm could it cause to anyone? If I had seen a sea fairy who said to me, "Don't grieve, Captain. You have a better world before you—a world with a happy, loving woman who will be a companion to her man, not his slave, a world with a man worthy of such a woman, a world with happy, well-fed, well-dressed, well-loved children not bereft of shelter . . . "

The port exorcist put a bowl full of water in front of me and said his chants and adjured the mermaid to leave me alone. He tied a talisman to my arm and said, "The mermaid has agreed to leave you alone." Contrary to his wishes, I wanted her to come at least once a day and meet me on the water. The port exorcist said, "Listen to me, Captain. Go look for work." But I was in no mood for work. Besides, what would I do? Everyone said, "Make a fresh start." But how? I had lost all my capital. Fatigue had overcome me, as if I had carried the world on my shoulders. I'd become so impatient that I couldn't bear the noise and the heat. Every evening, I'd sit on the beach, hoping that the mermaid would slip away from her brothers and come to see me.

The savage beat of the drums, the swaying of heads and bodies, the words of the songs—I spun around and retched. Someone is rubbing my shoulders. I look and see it's Rostam. It feels like a cool breeze is blowing inside me. I ask, "Rostam where have you been all this time that you haven't come to see your captain? Why should you be jealous of the mermaid? Listen, you idiot . . . " Rostam looks at me sadly and says nothing. I wish the mermaid would come. I'd lay my head in her lap, on her shimmering scales, and weep. She'd wipe my tears away and say, "You're tired. The tempestuous life you've led has worn you out. How old are you that you're so broken?" I said, "I must be sixty, but according to my birth certificate I'm fifty-eight. Mr. Daneshmand got it for me. I studied six classes in his school." God rest his soul! Where is he now? The mermaid asked, "Have you studied geography, too?" I said, "I liked geography more than any other subject." She said, "I've seen the sky many times. It looks so much like the sea. The stars sparkle just like pieces of shell and the crescent of the moon is like a ship." She said, "I come to the surface at night."

Her brothers came home in the evening empty-handed, and said, "We smell a human." The mermaid hid me under a cluster of sea-fern and started telling her brothers the story of a man who had hunted a whale. Rebuking them, she asked, "Are you less than human that you can't hunt a miserable shark?" Her voice was like the murmur of water, of the breeze, of the rustling of leaves . . . In the prison of Borazjan, Taher Khan used to say, "Man the coward." The mermaid then turned to her brothers and asked, "Do you remember great-grandfather used to say, 'There was a man who drowned his wife and children in the sea so he could turn his attention to fighting his enemies who had come from the other end of the world—fought them and threw them all into the sea'? Do you remember great-grandfather used to say, 'The man had only a simple grey shirt on and a loincloth, and tied a string around his waist, while all his companions wore brocade'?" There, under the sea-fern, I vowed to myself that one day I'd get permission from the mermaid to go to Bushehr, look for the giant cypress that's a memorial to Mir Mohanna, and light a candle for him in the sanctuary of the tree trunk. She told her brothers, "You should be ashamed of yourselves. Hunt that shark down by any means." The brothers said, "First we must deal with the human."

They found me under the sea-fern. I punched one brother in the abdomen and, grabbing the knife under the sea-fern, put it to the throat of the second. The third ran away.

The day that I put the knife to Jerry's throat . . . Jerry had become lord and master of the island. He'd learned Persian, too. He'd made the islanders his servants and peasants. The queen had charged him to build houses. The first one he'd built for himself on the choicest part of the beach. I was there to load red ocher. I needed to hire a few laborers. There were only nine of us, and if we didn't get help, it would be night and we'd be late reaching our destination. The laborers said, "Mr. Jerry should give permission." "And who is this Mr. Jerry?" I asked. They said, "He's lord of the island and has high connections. We don't take a drink of water without his permission. Besides, fresh water must come from Bandar Abbas. Four *rial*s a bucket. Bandar Abbas itself doesn't have very good water. Kan has fresh water, but there's always something wrong. They've been saying for the past five years they're going to build a dam on the river Minab and bring drinking water to the port, but nothing has happened. We won't see it in our lifetime." "What's happened to the Portuguese well?" I asked. "Dried up," they said. I said, "Toss down a piece of felt into the well. When it gets wet, pull it up and suck on it." They said, "The bottom of the well is so dry it's cracked." "What does Jerry do?" I asked. "Drinks beer from cans," they said.

I went with the laborers to see Jerry. He was sitting on a rattan chair on the veranda of his house, smoking a pipe. His eyes were blue, his hair the color of ripened wheat, and his face, neck, and arms were copper-colored. One of the laborers said, "Mr. Jerry, Captain Abdol wants to hire us to load red ocher. He's going to Pakistan. He's got the papers, too." Jerry bellowed, "Kaptin Abtul, kiss my ass! You itiots und ninkoompoops go to boats? Tomorrow race. Atmiral kom vatch. Televishun kom make film. I say hank brocade koortin over head." One of the laborers said, "Mr. Jerry, I looked but couldn't find a brocade curtain. Can't you have a race without a brocade curtain?" Jerry put his pipe down on the table near him and stood up. He punched the laborer in the gut so hard that he fell to the ground. I pulled out my switchblade, released the catch, and called, *"Ya Ali!"* I put the knife to Jerry's throat. His blue eyes blinked and he kicked me in the shin. I said, "You son of a bitch. Captain Abdol kiss your ass? I'll show you now. Who the fuck are you anyway? Your queen—" I wish I'd killed him. The laborers overwhelmed me. Because of Jerry's complaint I was taken to Borazjan prison for the second time. Taher Khan was still there, now old and bent. But the sayyid had been granted an amnesty—some celebration or other. For fear of Jerry, the laborers didn't testify that he had hit their mate, but they also didn't testify that I had put the knife to his throat. I spent three months in prison. Taher Khan's eyes were very dim, and he couldn't read books himself anymore. He'd asked for glasses, but no one had come to his help. I read aloud to him. He spoke of Gandhi. He said, "That half-naked, frail man, that man who's wasted his body to awaken his nation—he's burned like a candle so his people will be illuminated." "Captain," he said, "Gandhi is the Buddha of our time. Don't take him lightly." He'd sigh and continue, "People aren't mistaken. They know their man.

They single out a man, get fascinated by him, and salute him. Maybe they don't really know the reason for this choice or this fascination, but they're not wrong. I salute those people who are right." When I got out of prison, I bought Taher Khan a pair of glasses. I hope they're right for his eyes.

The mermaid gave me a plank. I recognized it; it was from my launch. She said, "Quick, get away." The sun had risen and the wind was blowing landward from the sea.

A fisherman found me lying on the shore. I could only open a corner of one eye. He had rolled up his pants. "It's Captain Abdol!" he shouted. "It's the man himself!" The fishermen gathered around me. I felt them carrying me. When I came to, I was lying under the shade of a straw shack. The sun was glaring in my eyes. The air was humid and sticky. One moment my body would be wet, the next it would be dry, and again wet. I could smell the sea menstruating. The fisherman's wife was sitting on the ground, suckling her newborn. I remembered the monkey I had left behind in Madras. He'd go begging, putting one hand over his eyes and holding out the other to people. The woman's breasts were brown and small. The children were milling about their mother, and the flies . . . the woman put her baby on the ground. She got up and poured me tea and gave me back my clothes to put on. My jacket was hanging from the peg and my compass was in the pocket.

I'm foaming at the mouth, retching, retching. Rostam is wiping my face and beard with a wet handkerchief. My head feels empty. I close my eyes. The poison in my body must have left. I've sprouted wings and am rising toward the sky. I go up. The night is bright and the sky is littered with pieces of shell-star and the ship of the crescent moon. I'm sitting in the heavenly ship, steering toward the earth. A certain mood has come over me that I've never felt before. Seems like all the world, with all its oceans and all its mermaids, belongs to me. Seems like a woman, who looks like the mermaid, is fanning my soul with a fan made of sandalwood. The woman's glance is full of understanding and love and joy. In the sparkle of her eyes there's no grief or poverty or anxiety. I say, "Hello, woman, where've you been all this time?"

Seems like all the fish, corals, ferns, and the vastness of the sea and land and sky belong to me. Seems like someone has washed and burnished my soul. Ecstasy, joy, bliss; I should sit down one day and gather together such words. I used to sit with Taher Khan in the prison and collect words together. Once we made a list of words that mean sorrow. The words stretched as far as hell itself. Oh, woe!

My eyes are closed and I see a brilliant light in front of my eyes that I've never seen before. I look closely and see a big garden where everything—flowers, fruits, trees, branches, stems, blacks, palm trees, lotuses—all are made of light. The water is light, the rocks are light, sky and earth are light. The gleam grows brighter and brighter. I open my eyes. An Indian friend puts a piece of paper in front of me and gives me a pencil. I close my eyes again.

Listen and write:

"You didn't have a compass with you, so you struggled with the waves. Darkness and loneliness and separation stared you in the face. You panicked. But you struggled and got yourself ashore. May the compass always be with you, and your efforts be directed to an honorable shore! Thus struggling with eagerness, if death should snatch you, it will be with eagerness. Life is a struggle. May blood and honor be companions in your veins, and truth and righteousness the end of your struggle! Thus it was with Mohammad and Ali and Hosayn and Jesus and their peers, and thus it is with me, who is the lowliest of servants. Heed this advice and sample the wondrous pleasures of your manliness, for they have sampled it and their righteousness and convictions, after they were gone, have continued to endure, standing prophet-like as a testimony to the vitality of their faith. What fear now if ashes were thrown over their comely faces, or someone poured impurity into my beggar's bowl, or the one bore his cross on his shoulder, or the other died a thirsty martyr—thirst and satiety to him were the same. Theirs was bliss, the companion of their days and nights when their convictions were taking form. With lives in hand, their tongues uttered, 'O faith, bestow certitude upon us.'

"A day will come when certainties will freely translate into action. Tyrants will be withheld from tyranny. Sorrow-laden words will find no meaning in the world. Await the world in which men, women, and children will not be images of pain, where they will no longer be clothed in grief, agitation, helplessness, forbearance, and silence, where the free-spirited will not rot like caterpillars in their cocoons—amid all their wealth. Such a world will come to be.

"Put together another launch. Equipped and assured with faith, set off once again, for the objective is to travel, not to arrive. Life is a journey, short or long; what is important is being on the move. You may well be led astray, or brought down to your knees, or wearied with the dead ends and the ups and downs, or jolted hard at the turns. Beware lest these jolts lessen the vigor of body and soul, or dim the light of your spirit in the vessel of your frame, for the highway lies before you and the way, safe and shady and tree-lined, is apparent. Then set off, traveler. *Charai vati.*"

Everything is wrapped in silence. I open my eyes. My Indian friend takes the paper from me, kisses it, and lays it on his eyes. Other Indian friends surround him to hear the message. I test ecstasy. Rostam takes my arm and helps me up. Baba Zar stands up, too, and fixes his eye upon mine and says, "God be thanked, your rider has dismounted." A woman says, "Congratulations to you! You've entered the circle of the 'airy.'"

I hold Rostam's hand and ask, "Rostam, was Taher Khan here? I heard his voice."

He says, "No, Taher Khan wasn't here."

I say, "Rostam. I set you free. From now on you're free as the birds in the air." Rostam laughs.

I say, "It's clear as day to me that Taher Khan's followers are waiting for me. I'll set off first thing tomorrow morning."

SIMIN DANESHVAR was born in 1921 in Shiraz, Iran. With the exception of two years spent at Stanford University as a Fulbright Scholar, she has remained in Iran, where she lives and writes today. She has published numerous short stories and a major best-selling novel, *Savushun* (1969), which has sold over half a million copies in Iran and become the most-read Persian novel of all time. Her most recent work is *Island of Wandering*, a trilogy of novels set in Iran before, during, and after the Islamic Revolution. It will be published in English by Mage in 1995.

HASAN JAVADI was born in 1938 in Tabriz, Iran. He received his Ph.D. in English Literature from Cambridge University. His books include *Satire in Persian Literature* (Dickinson, 1988) and Gholam Hosayn Sa'edi's *Dandil* (Random House, 1981).

AMIN NESHATI received his masters degree in English from Boston College. He lives in Annandale, Virginia, where he is the assistant editor of the *Journal of Iranian Studies*. He was the co-translator of *Taj al Saltana, Crowning Anguish: Memoirs of a Persian Princess from the Harem to Modernity* (Mage, 1993).

The jacket illustration is an opaque watercolor attributed to the seventeenth-century Persian painter Mohammad-Sharif Musavvar. The original painting is now at the Arthur M. Sackler Gallery in Washington, D.C. The Persian calligraphy for the story titles is by A.H. Tabnak. The text type is a digitized version of Janson, a typeface long thought to have been made by the Dutchman Anton Janson, a type founder practicing in Leipzig during the years 1668–1687. However, this type is actually the work of Nicholas Kis (1650–1702), a Hungarian, who most probably learned his trade from the Dutch type founder Dirk Voskens. The display face is Medici Script, designed by Hermann Zapf in 1971 for Linotype. The type was set in-house by Bill Henry using FrameMaker 4.0 and Quark XPress 3.3 on an Apple Macintosh Quadra 900. Thomson-Shore output, printed and bound the book in Dexter, Michigan. The book was designed by Mohammad and Najmieh Batmanglij.